Body at the Bakery

NIGHTMARE ARIZONA
PARANORMAL COZY MYSTERIES

BETH DOLGNER

Body at the Bakery
Nightmare, Arizona Paranormal Cozy Mysteries, Book Ten
© 2025 Beth Dolgner

ISBN-13: 978-1-958587-31-7

Published by Redglare Press
Cover by Dark Mojo Designs
Print Formatting by The Madd Formatter

https://bethdolgner.com

CHAPTER ONE

"I think it's bigger."

"It's the same size as yesterday."

"And the day before."

"No, it's bigger! I'm sure of it." Maida reached out a small hand and held it up near the shimmering red and gold egg. "See? It's even taller than the tips of my fingers now."

The other two witches both leaned toward the gilt bird-cage, trying to make their own comparison.

"She's right," said Madge. She straightened up and gracefully pushed her long blonde curls over her shoulder. A smile played on her lips, which made her look even more beautiful.

"Hmm." Morgan squinted as she pushed her wrinkled face closer to the egg. "Yes, I suppose there has been some progress. Excellent."

Maida dropped her hand, and the three witches stepped away from the cage. It had been two weeks since Baxter had spontaneously combusted, his phoenix form exploding into a ball of flame, then crumbling into ashes. Not long after, an egg had begun to emerge from the ash pile. The red and gold swirls on the shell had a reflective quality, giving the egg a magical-looking sheen.

Since the egg had first appeared, it had been the center of attention at Nightmare Sanctuary Haunted House.

For Justine, who was trying to manage the year-round haunted attraction and all its staff, it had become a bit of a challenge. She was sitting next to me on a bench at one of the tables set in neat rows along the expanse of the Sanctuary's dining room. "We're three minutes late already," she said, looking impatiently at her watch. "Baxter isn't going to hatch just yet, so let's get started."

Justine stood and began to make her way to the podium at one end of the dining room, and everyone who was still gathered around the birdcage took that as their cue to sit down. The witches slid onto a bench one table over, and Mori settled next to me, her purple silk gown rustling with the gentle movement.

"Every evening when I wake up, I worry I've missed the big event," Mori said. She looked at me with her exotic burnt-orange eyes while patting a hand against her black hair, which was twisted up into an especially tall coiffure. "And, just in case I wake up to find everyone celebrating, I make sure to look ready for the party."

I grinned at Mori. "I can't wait for Baxter to hatch, either. I told Damien that if the egg starts to crack, he has to call me immediately. I don't care if it's four in the morning."

"Four o'clock would be great," Mori said, "since that's well before sunrise." As one of the Sanctuary's two resident vampires, she was inside her coffin in the basement by the time the sun rose over Nightmare, Arizona, every day.

I felt pressure against my lower back, and I twisted around to see Felipe, Mori's pet chupacabra, with his front paws pressed against me. He lifted his gray, leathery snout toward my face hopefully, and I obliged by scratching him behind the ears.

"We're all looking forward to the egg hatching," Justine

called in a loud voice from the podium. Mori and I dutifully turned our attention to her. "So, here's what we're going to do: we are officially on baby phoenix watch. Someone will always have eyes on the egg, even while the haunt is open. The second something begins to happen, the watcher will send a group text to alert everyone."

There was a murmur of approval from the staff, then Justine continued. "The tourist season is wrapping up soon, so be thinking about some fun ways we can promote the Sanctuary and bring in as much business as possible over the summer months."

I made a quiet noise of dread, and Mori snickered. "You'll survive," she whispered.

I was not looking forward to my first full summer in the desert. Even though everyone assured me Nightmare's higher elevation meant it wouldn't be as hot as it would be in places like Phoenix, I still figured anything that ranged into the triple digits was too hot.

Justine was already moving on to more announcements while I was picturing myself slowly melting into a puddle, my supernatural friends all standing around me and lamenting that none of their abilities had been able to keep me cool enough in the Arizona sun.

When I heard Justine say my name, I snapped back to the present moment and was pleased to hear her announce I would be in the lagoon vignette that night. I typically spent about half my nights working there, and the other half taking tickets at the front door. I enjoyed doing both, but after a relatively quiet day, I was in the mood to scare some tourists.

I made a beeline for the costume room as soon as Justine wrapped up the meeting, and before long, I was in my usual pirate costume. My long red coat and lacy black cuffs would be warm in the summer months, but at the moment, the ensemble felt great. Tall brown boots and a black tricorn hat completed the look, and I gave myself an appreciative glance in the mirror as I added makeup so my face would stand out in the dim lighting of the lagoon vignette.

Felipe was just bounding out of the dining room as I walked down the hallway that led from the costume room to the wide entryway that divided the east and west wings of the Sanctuary. The east wing of the former hospital building housed the staff-only areas, like offices and the dining room that we used for meetings. The haunt itself wound through the west wing of the building. Upstairs, many of the Sanctuary's residents lived in apartments that had once been hospital rooms.

I stopped and watched as Felipe ran along the hallway, his claws making their distinctive *tick-tack* sound on the stone floor.

"Shall we?" I heard a voice say from my immediate right.

I jumped and let out the smallest of shrieks. "Theo, you sneaky pirate!"

Theo puffed out his chest and lifted his chin. His pirate coat was much more elaborate than mine, and with his long brown hair and a mischievous glint in his brown eyes, he looked every bit the part. Except, to amp up the scare factor, Theo added zombie makeup.

Theo had been a real swashbuckler a couple hundred years before. His pirate swagger was authentic.

Theo chuckled at my startled reaction, but since his fangs had been filed down by a vampire hunter, his teeth gave no indication of his supernatural status. He held out his arm, and I looped mine through it. We had to walk single-file once we reached what we called the tunnels, the network of behind-the-scenes pathways between the different vignettes in the haunt.

We emerged through a door into the lagoon vignette.

4

Seraphina was already in her water tank, swimming somersaults as her silver tail flashed under the bright overhead lights. Beside her glass-fronted tank was the prop pirate ship. I always thought it was a shame the lights in the room were so dim once we opened for the evening, because it meant visitors couldn't fully appreciate the detail work on the ship. It did, I supposed, look a lot more scary in the near-dark.

Seraphina's head broke the surface of the water. "Fifteen days," she called to us.

"Isn't that the name of a zombie movie?" Theo asked. He struck a dramatic pose. "They should have cast me in it."

"No, you're thinking of *Twenty-Eight*—" I began, then waved him off. "Seraphina, what happens in fifteen days?"

Seraphina pushed some of her wet golden hair off her face, which had a pale green tone to it. "That's the average time it takes for a phoenix egg to hatch."

"It's been two weeks since Baxter burned," I noted. "Sounds like he could hatch any day now. But how did you find that out? I haven't been able to dig up anything online."

Seraphina waved a hand. "The library."

The corners of my lips turned down. "But we scoured the Sanctuary library and didn't find more than a few sentences about phoenixes."

"I know, but I was convinced there had to be something there. Earlier today, I talked Fiona into climbing up the ladder so she could look at the very top shelf again."

I suppressed a shiver as I pictured the rickety ladder attached to the railing along the library's shelves. "She's braver than me."

"Anyway, Fi got high enough that she could see there was a sort of hidden shelf up there. It's not very deep or tall, and it only has enough space to lay a few books on their side. So, when you're standing on the ground, it's completely hidden by the books on the shelf below it."

Theo and I were both leaning forward in anticipation. "And she found a book about phoenixes on the hidden shelf?" he asked.

Seraphina's head bobbled in something between a nod and a shake. "Sort of. It was a handwritten volume, apparently compiled by Baxter himself. He must have been doing research on his own kind for decades, and he put everything he learned into that book. The first entry dated from the thirties. The eighteen thirties, that is."

The awed expressions Theo and I gave Seraphina were exactly the reaction she wanted, judging by the way she beamed at us. "Baxter wrote that the usual time from combustion to hatching is about fifteen days. And, once he hatches, we're to feed him carrot shavings, orange rinds, and meatballs rolled in cinnamon."

I scrunched up my nose while Theo said, "I'd eat that. If I could eat."

"Fi found something else, too," Seraphina said hesitantly.

"What?" I asked.

"I thought Damien would have told you about it…" Seraphina shifted her gaze away from me, looking uncomfortable.

"He wasn't in his office when I got to work, and he didn't mention anything at lunch," I said.

"Fi only found the hidden shelf a couple hours ago, so he didn't know about it then, but…" Seraphina hesitated, then said, "In addition to Baxter's phoenix book, there was a diary. It was Lucille's."

I gasped, then immediately yanked up a sleeve of my pirate coat to look at my watch.

"Go," Theo commanded. "We can hold down the ship without you for a bit."

"Thanks!" I hollered over my shoulder as I ran toward the door to the tunnels.

By the time I reached Damien's office, I was out of breath, and I could feel a sheen of sweat on my forehead. I pulled off my tricorn hat, gave my auburn hair a shake, then banged on Damien's door. "It's me," I added.

A few seconds later, Damien opened the door. My boyfriend usually looked confident, but in that moment, he seemed shaken. His hair was tousled, like he'd been nervously running his fingers through the light-brown waves, and his tanned skin looked paler than usual.

Plus, his green eyes were glowing, which always indicated Damien's emotions were heightened.

"Sera told me about your mom's diary," I said. I stepped over the threshold and took Damien's hands in my own.

Damien's voice was heavy as he said, "We've been assuming my mother shed her human form because she was becoming too powerful, or too dangerous. As it turns out, she did it to protect me."

CHAPTER TWO

"Your mom ceased to exist in human form as a way to protect you?" I repeated. Lucille had been an enormously powerful psychic, and we had always assumed she had found a way to shed her mortal body either to keep herself from becoming too dangerous or to keep herself from being preyed on by people who would want to harness her power for themselves.

Damien nodded slowly. "She realized early on that I was going to be powerful, too. How could I not be, right? I'm the son of a phoenix and a psychic. She wrote that she had always worried she might be a target, and she realized I might be at risk, too. She didn't want someone to take me for my abilities. So, she found a way to protect me psychically. It would delay the onset of my true power, to help keep me off anyone's radar."

I shut my eyes briefly. "That helps explain why you didn't begin exhibiting signs of your abilities until you were a bit older." In fact, Damien's power had first manifested when he was saving Zach, the Sanctuary's werewolf accountant, from a bunch of bullies at high school.

Damien pulled his hands away from mine so he could shut and lock his office door. He wordlessly returned to his desk and pulled a worn black leather journal toward him.

He opened to a page he had marked with a scrap of paper, then handed it to me.

What will be left of me? read the firm, feminine handwriting. *Some bit of a specter will remain, perhaps, or maybe nothing at all. But my son will be safe, and that's all that matters.*

I had difficulty reading the last few words because of the tears forming in my eyes. Slowly, I put the journal down. "Oh, Damien," I whispered. "The psychic protection took everything she had. She loved you so much."

"She still does," Damien said, his voice thick. I glanced over to see his eyes turned toward the ceiling. Lucille's ghost—or specter, as she had put it in her diary—had begun making her presence known in the past year, though we never knew where or when she would turn up.

I moved closer to Damien and wrapped my arms around his waist. His arms slid around my shoulders, and he buried his face against the top of my head.

We stood like that for a while, not needing to say anything to each other, until Damien let out something like a laugh mixed with a sigh. "Aren't you supposed to be scaring people right now?"

"After Seraphina told me about the diary, I wanted to check on you," I said, my voice muffled against the jacket of Damien's charcoal-gray suit. "You weren't here when I got to work, so I assume you were at home, trying to absorb the news."

I felt Damien's head nodding. "Yeah. I'm sorry I didn't tell you, but I needed some time to myself to let it all sink in."

I loosened my grip on Damien and took half a step away so I could look up at him. "This helps explain why your dad was so intent on teaching you to hide your abilities once they began to manifest."

Damien's eyes took on an unfocused look, and I knew

he was remembering Baxter's mysterious but intense insistence that Damien should bury his supernatural talents. "He didn't want my mother's sacrifice to be for nothing. Her spell kept my abilities suppressed for years, and when they started to show, he taught me to repress them." Damien sighed heavily. "I wish he would have told me why he wanted me to act like a normal, totally human kid. It would have made for a much better relationship between us."

"He was trying to protect you," I said. "Not just from people who might take you, but from any guilt you might feel knowing your mom sacrificed herself for you."

"I do feel guilty, so my father was right about that," Damien conceded. "At the same time, though, I'm grateful I had such a loving mother."

"You and Baxter are going to have a lot to discuss after he hatches," I noted.

"Hatches, and turns into a human again," Damien corrected. "And while we wait for those things to happen, I've promised Tanner and McCrory we'd visit that energy spring my father used to take them to every year. Would you like to join us for that after we close for the night?"

I quickly agreed, since I was curious to see the spot for myself. The Sanctuary's resident ghosts were so vivid that sometimes they appeared almost as living humans—albeit ones who glowed and could walk through walls—and they attributed it to the fact that Baxter used to take them to a spot near Nightmare that had concentrated psychic energy. I knew people flocked to similar spots up in Sedona, where they were called energy vortexes, and I was looking forward to testing my ability to feel the energy.

"Now go be a menacing pirate," Damien said. He gave me a quick kiss, and I had to rub some dark-red lipstick off his lips before I left. I glanced back as I closed his office door behind me and was relieved to see a small smile on his face.

I gave Theo and Seraphina a quick update in between groups of visitors coming through the lagoon. It was a Wednesday night, our slowest of the week, so it wasn't hard to do.

After the Sanctuary closed at midnight, I changed into the jeans and black Nightmare Sanctuary hoodie I had worn to work, then returned to Damien's office. He was just pulling a worn wooden box out of its spot in his desk drawer.

"You've got their guns, but where are the ghosts?" I asked. The ghosts of Butch Tanner and Connor McCrory were tethered to the six-shooters they had used in their legendary—and fatal—shootout on High Noon Boulevard. Every day, costumed actors re-created the scene several times for the tourists who came to Nightmare for its Wild West history.

Damien turned to a panel on the wall behind him, where tarnished brass buttons had a handwritten label next to each one. The old-fashioned call system had been used during the Sanctuary's days as a hospital, but it still worked. And, somehow, it had been rigged to call the ghosts, wherever they might be in the building.

A few seconds after Damien pressed the button for Tanner and McCrory, the ghosts of the outlaw and the sheriff sailed through the wall next to Damien's door.

"We were right in the middle of checking on the egg," Tanner said, his eyes glinting above the red bandana he wore over his mouth and nose.

"It's getting bigger. I'm sure of it." McCrory gave his black duster a shake and lifted his matching hat. "Miss Olivia, ma'am."

"Good evening, gentlemen. Are you excited?"

"Relieved is more like it," McCrory answered. "It's

been well over a year since we last visited the spring, and Tanner and I have both agreed we're feeling a bit weak. I haven't felt this way since before Baxter brought us home from the antique store."

"Let's get going," Tanner said. "I'm riding shotgun!"

Tanner was already on the move before I could tell him the passenger seat of Damien's Corvette was my spot. Damien grabbed the six-shooter box, since the guns had to go wherever the ghosts wanted to go, and we took off after Tanner. McCrory brought up the rear.

There was a bit of grumbling from Tanner when I shooed him out of the passenger seat, but he relented and joined McCrory just behind Damien and me. As Damien pulled out of the dirt parking lot, the car's headlights swept across the time-darkened stone of the Sanctuary.

This building wouldn't look nearly as spooky if someone took a pressure-washer to the facade, I thought.

Damien slowly navigated the narrow dirt lane that led from the front of the Sanctuary to the street, then brought his car to a stop when we reached the crossroads. The waning moon illuminated the old gallows that stood there, and no matter how many times I had walked or driven past them, they still made my skin crawl.

"Which way, gentlemen?" Damien asked.

"Right," Tanner said at the same time McCrory said, "Straight."

"We can get there either way," Tanner said with a dismissive sniff.

"We'll go right, then," Damien said. As he pressed the gas pedal and turned onto the street, he added, "And then what?"

"You'll want to turn left in about a mile," McCrory said.

"Three miles, at least," Tanner argued.

"No way is it that far."

"No way is it that close."

I pressed my lips together to keep from laughing.

"Just tell me when we reach the right street," Damien said. He glanced at me. "I wish Fiona had found a map up on that hidden library shelf, too."

"That wouldn't be any fun."

It took four wrong turns, two arguments between the ghosts, and something that Tanner swore was an attempt to exorcise McCrory, but eventually, Damien pulled over to the side of a narrow gravel road that wound through a hilly, forested area. As forested as things got around Nightmare, anyway. There were scrawny palo verdes, mesquites, and ironwood trees, all standing tall above bushy plants that I didn't know the names for yet. All I knew about them was that I had to watch my step, because they had thorns.

The ghosts were especially visible out in the dark night, far away from the lights of the town, and they led the way down a path that was nearly overgrown. They moved so quickly they were soon out of sight around a bend, and Damien and I had to resort to using the flashlights on our cell phones so we could follow the trail.

After a short walk, Damien drew in a long, slow breath. "We're close. Can you feel it?"

"No," I said, disappointed. After landing in Nightmare and finding out the supernatural world was real, I had learned I was something called a conjuror. If I wanted something badly enough, I could make it happen. So, I focused all my desire on sensing the energy spring.

All I got was a slight tingle along my spine, but I took it as a good sign.

The ghosts were the real indicator of the vast amount of energy coming up through the earth. We could hear them whooping with delight before we could see them, and when they came into view, they were glowing so brightly I had to shade my eyes. McCrory was doing a little shuffle, while Tanner threw his hat into the air and turned in circles.

"They really are soaking up a lot of energy," I commented. "I wonder if we could bring your mom here?"

Damien had slid on his mirrored sunglasses. Usually, he did that to hide his eyes when they were glowing, but I knew he was doing it at that moment to cut the glare from the ghosts. "That's a great idea, but we have to find her first. She always pops up somewhere unexpected."

"That little psychic girl can invite her," McCrory suggested.

Lucille's great-niece—and Damien's cousin—was beginning to explore her own psychic abilities, which seemed to run in the family. Lately, Lucy had been visited by her great-aunt Lucille in dreams, and once, Lucille had communicated during a lesson from Vivian, the Sanctuary's psychic and Lucy's new tutor.

Damien and I agreed that was a good idea, and he suggested we go talk to Mama the next day. Since she was Lucille's sister and Lucy's grandmother, Damien and I liked to consult with Mama on anything having to do with the family.

"I'll grab a box of cinnamon rolls beforehand," I offered. "Those always make her happy."

So, the next morning, I woke up and made the short drive to Bake in the Day, which was on High Noon Boulevard. Since that street had been covered over with dirt to look more like it had in the eighteen hundreds, cars weren't allowed on it. I parked one street over, instead.

Both sides of High Noon Boulevard were lined with a covered boardwalk, so when I reached the street, I stepped up onto the wooden boards and headed for the bakery. I had never been there, myself, since it was usually Mama or Damien who picked up baked goods.

I was only a few steps away from the bakery door when I heard raised voices. Two men were standing a short distance away, both glaring at each other. As I watched, one of them curled his hands into fists. "I'll be out of business in a month if you do that!"

CHAPTER THREE

"Don't be such a drama queen, Fred!"

I wasn't the only one staring at the two men who were arguing. People had stopped to see what would happen next, and the man named Fred suddenly seemed to realize it. Slowly, he uncurled his fists and stepped back from the other man.

"This isn't over, Jack," Fred said, much quieter this time but still loud enough for me to hear the anger and the implied threat. Without waiting for a response, Fred spun on the heel of his shiny brown cowboy boot and stalked away.

The people around me started moving again, and even Jack shook his head and walked away, so I closed the gap to the bakery door. When I opened it, the warm, sweet smell of fresh-baked pastries welcomed me.

There were a few small round tables in front of the windows, but the long display case at the back of the bakery took up the bulk of the small space. Even though it wasn't lunchtime yet, some of the baked goods appeared to be sold out already.

"Hi, welcome to Bake in the Day."

I looked up to see a short curvy woman who looked like she was in her mid-fifties. Her hair was pulled up under a bright-green scarf, which set off her sparkling hazel eyes. She propped her elbows on top of the display case and raised her eyebrows knowingly. "It's your first time here."

I smiled. "How did you know?"

The woman pointed her chin in the direction of a display of bagels, muffins, and scones. "First-timers get a look on their faces when they come in here. I like to think of it as childlike wonder."

"That's an accurate description for how I'm feeling," I admitted. "I'm Olivia. I rent an apartment over at Cowboy's Corral Motor Lodge. Mama Dalton swears by your cinnamon rolls."

"She's one of my favorite customers and a good friend. I'm Chelsea, and I know all about you and your skills for solving murders."

I must have looked surprised, because Chelsea quickly added, "Mama brags about you."

"That's better than being the star of town gossip," I said lightly. I jerked a thumb over my shoulder. "Of course, with the argument that just happened right outside your door, I don't think anyone will be talking about me today."

Chelsea's welcoming smile faded, and she made a noise of disgust. "I'm glad those two stopped shouting. That kind of thing hurts sales." She waved a hand around the empty bakery. "I had half a dozen people in here, but they all went outside to watch the show."

"One of them—I think his name was Fred—was saying something about going out of business."

"Fred Corcoran. Lots of folks call him The General, since he's the manager of the Nightmare General Store. He's as upset as the rest of us that Jack Wiley wants to hike up our rent yet again. And right at the end of tourist season, no less!"

I nodded as the exchange I'd witnessed between the

two men suddenly made a lot more sense. "Jack is Fred's landlord."

"And mine, unfortunately." Chelsea blew out a frustrated breath. "My sales are already starting to dip. I joke that for every five degrees the daily temperature goes up, my sales go down by five percent. It's not far from the truth, though."

"I work at Nightmare Sanctuary, and our manager, Justine, recently mentioned we need to brainstorm ways to bring in more people during the summer. I just came to Nightmare at the end of August last year, so I'm not sure what to expect for my first full summer here."

"Hot. Dry. Quiet. Most tourists are smart enough to visit cooler places in the summer months. I make enough money to get me through the off-season, but a raise in my rent is really going to hurt."

"How many buildings does Jack own?"

"He's got a couple of places in the New Downtown, but they cater to locals, so their business tends to be steadier all year long. The rent hikes don't hit them quite as hard." Chelsea's shop was located where Nightmare had gotten its start, but as the old mining town had transformed into a tourist town, most local businesses had moved to a different area. Even though that had happened half a century before, it was still known as the New Downtown.

"Well, I'm going to do my small part in helping with those rent payments," I said. "I'd like a dozen cinnamon rolls, please."

"Coming right up." Chelsea's smile returned, and she grabbed a white pastry box. As she filled the box, her smile faded again, replaced by a thoughtful look. "You know, if we all just stood up to Jack, maybe we could do something about it. He can't make money if we've all gone out of business, and maybe we can get him to understand that."

Chelsea closed the box, set it on the counter, and moved over to the cash register as I pulled bills out of my wallet. "You didn't know your cinnamon rolls were going to come with a side of whining, did you? Sorry about that."

"It's fine. I completely understand your frustration. And, hopefully, you're right that Jack might see reason. It would be foolish of him to get so greedy that he winds up owning nothing but a bunch of empty storefronts."

"You get it." Chelsea handed me my change, followed by the box. "Nice meeting you, Olivia. You tell Mama I said hey."

I promised to do just that and headed out, feeling grateful I didn't have to worry about things like rent hikes. My little efficiency apartment at Cowboy's Corral wasn't much, but I got the place in exchange for doing marketing work for the motel. It was a deal for me and Mama, who ran the motel along with her husband, Benny.

Cowboy's Corral Motor Lodge was less than a mile from High Noon Boulevard. It had been built in the nineteen sixties, back in the heyday of road trips and roadside attractions. A vintage neon sign in front of the two-story cinderblock office had the motel's name along with a snoozing cowboy with his hat pulled down over his face. The entrance to the parking lot was on one side of the office, and the exit was on the other.

I parked in the back right corner of the motel, since my apartment was at the top of the staircase there. There were two wings of the motel, which ran back from the street, and being so far from passing cars meant my place was nice and quiet at night. Not that there was a lot of traffic when I got home from the Sanctuary around one o'clock in the morning, of course.

With the box of cinnamon rolls in hand, I walked up to the office just in time to see Damien climbing out of his car. He came over and wished me a good morning before giving me a light kiss. "Shall we?" he asked, opening the glass door of the office for me.

Mama was watering a few potted plants as we walked in, and she turned at the sound of the bell over the door. She smiled broadly at us, and then her eyes moved to the box in my hands. "You brought me cinnamon rolls." Her eyebrows drew down.

I stared at Mama stupidly for a moment. "But," I stammered, "I thought you loved these."

"I do." Mama put down her watering can and crossed her arms. She was frowning at Damien and me, but I could also see the amusement in her brilliant blue eyes. "You two only bring me these when there's bad news or you need to butter me up."

"We've only done that once," Damien protested.

"Still, I know you're here to ask for something." Mama had a way of knowing things. While her sister, Lucille, had been a full-blown psychic, Mama had buried her burgeoning abilities when she was a preteen. She had wanted nothing more than a normal life, but some of her heightened senses were impossible to tamp down.

"Grab a roll and sit down," Damien said.

"Uh-oh. It's bad news, then." Mama kept her eyes on Damien's face as she reached out and took a roll.

Once we were all seated in the saggy chairs in front of the check-in desk, Damien said, "I wouldn't call it bad news. But we learned something significant about my mom."

Mama had just taken a bite of cinnamon roll, and she hurriedly chewed and swallowed. "Tell me."

Damien looked at me, and I took his hand. He squeezed my fingers, then hesitantly told Mama about Lucille's diary and the news that she had given up her human form to protect Damien.

I'm not sure what kind of a reaction I had been expecting, but it wasn't the quiet response Mama gave when Damien had finished. "Of course," she said.

"Wait. You already knew?" Damien asked.

"I didn't know for a fact, but I *knew*." Mama touched a finger to her fluffy gray hair. "Even back then, more than forty years ago, I had my suspicions that Lucille's exit from this world was somehow tied to you, Damien. Baxter refused to say if my guess was right, but I figured she was trying to protect you, somehow. It's one of the reasons I was such a pain in your rear when you were a kid."

Damien's shoulders relaxed, and he smiled sadly. "I thought you were just a nosy lady who couldn't stand misbehaving kids." Mama had notoriously yelled at Damien when he was causing trouble with some other boys, but at the time, Damien hadn't known she was his aunt, since Baxter had cut ties with Lucille's side of the family.

"Last night, we took Tanner and McCrory to a spot in Nightmare that has a concentrated energy of some sort," I said. "McCrory suggested we take Lucille there for a spiritual boost, too. We thought Lucy could invite her the next time Lucille shows up in her mind."

"It can't hurt to ask," Mama said. "I remember Sheriff McCrory talking about that spring, years ago. This would be before you were born, Damien. He'd come back from there bright as day and more flirtatious than ever. He's the only ghost who's ever hit on me, you know."

The door opened just then, and Mama clamped her lips together. It wasn't a motel guest coming through the door but Emmett Kline, the real estate agent who had helped with a couple of murder investigations in Nightmare and had recently admitted to being in the know about the supernatural. As usual, he was dressed in an expensive-looking suit. This time, it was a dark-brown one with a coordinating paisley tie.

"Well, I get to see two of the people on my list with one visit!" Emmett smoothed a hand over his slicked-back white hair. "And I get to see my favorite amateur sleuth."

"What can we do for you, Emmett?" Mama asked as Damien offered up a cinnamon roll.

Emmett gratefully accepted the roll, but he was waving his hand around so dramatically that bits of cinnamon sugar went flying through the air. "The Nightmare Historic Society needs you! And by 'you,' I mean you, Mama, and you, Damien."

"Aw, I feel left out," I said, laughing.

"We're collecting raffle prizes for our annual fundraiser. I was hoping you two would contribute."

"You know I always donate something," Mama said. "Let me finish this roll, and then I'll grab you a gift certificate for a couple free nights at the motel."

"Your dad, Damien, used to dig up interesting old things for the historic society," Emmett said pointedly.

"I'll dig up something, as well," Damien promised.

"Emmett, you know everyone in this town," I said as Emmett finally stopped waving his cinnamon roll around and began to eat it. "What do you know about Jack, the landlord for the bakery and general store? I heard him and the manager of the general store getting into it today over a possible rent increase."

"Jack Wiley?" Emmett shrugged. "He's got a reputation for being a bad landlord. He won't do needed maintenance, and he likes to crank up the rent without warning. Most of my work is in residential properties, though, so I don't really know Jack except by reputation."

"Which, apparently, isn't a good one," I said.

"No. Jack drove two of my friends out of business with his rent prices. And you're not the only one who's seen The

General go after him. Fred once tried to kick him out of the general store, but Jack said Fred had no right to do that, since he owned the place. It got ugly before some folks finally separated the two of them."

Emmett dusted off his fingers and shook his head slowly. "Someday, karma is going to get Jack."

CHAPTER FOUR

Emmett didn't seem to realize just how ominous his words sounded, because he shifted right to giving a sly look to both Damien and me. "By the way," he said, "you two missed out on that fine piece of property out by the state park."

I couldn't help the laugh that erupted from my lips. "Emmett, you had a ghoul wandering around that property, and a villainous magician was camping there. Those are both deal-breakers."

"Whatever happened to the magician, anyway?"

I was still getting used to the notion that Emmett knew all about the supernatural world. No one had told him, but he'd gotten so many bizarre real estate requests from people who worked at the Sanctuary that he had finally put the pieces together himself. Most recently, Emmett had found someone wandering a large tract of land he was selling and recognized them as a ghoul. Emmett had then successfully gotten rid of it.

"We assume he went back to wherever he came from," Damien said. "I'm sure the Night Runners are angry that we found their treasure trove, but I'm hoping they're smart enough not to retaliate."

"We're all hoping that," I quipped.

When Baxter had gone missing a year before, it took a

long time to find any leads to his whereabouts. Finally, we learned he had been taken by the Night Runners, a faction that operated on the supernatural black market. Not only that, but they had been using a cave in the area to stash dark magical items as well as supernatural creatures they wanted in their possession. Baxter had been one of those creatures.

When we found the cave a couple weeks before, we had also rescued an emaciated vampire. Theo kept in touch with her, and she had recently texted to say she was feeling back to normal and happy to be with her enclave in California again.

"And I'm hoping for no more ghouls," Emmett said. "Yuck. Anyway, the mayor's daughter got the place. Says she's going to build a luxury campground for hikers."

"It will have great views," I said.

"You know, there's another place you two would love," Emmett began. "I'm not the one selling it, but I'd be happy to represent you two as buyers."

"We're not shopping for real estate," Damien said, looking torn between laughter and exasperation.

"It's historic. A great brick building, with an attic you could host a party in, it's so big."

"I don't need an attic at this time," I assured Emmett.

"It's zoned commercial and residential. You could live on the second story and open something on the ground floor. A mini Nightmare Sanctuary experience, maybe, or a gift shop for the haunted house! Or, if you prefer, become a landlord yourself and rent the place out."

Mama had gone behind the counter to get the promised gift certificate for Emmett, and she walked up to him and thrust it in front of his face. "Here you go," she said pointedly.

Emmett opened his mouth, looking like he wanted to keep trying to make a sale, but he wisely closed it and gave

Mama a peck on the cheek, instead. "Thank you, Mama. The Nightmare Historic Society appreciates your support."

"I'll let you know when I've found something to donate, too," Damien promised.

"Thanks. For the cinnamon roll and the donations." Emmett walked out, waving the gift certificate with as much flair as he'd been waving his roll earlier.

Mama mimed wiping sweat off her brow. "Whew! We got him out the door before he could talk you into a down-payment on a piece of real estate you don't even want."

"Good. I need to make a lot more money before I go buying old buildings." I suppressed a yawn. "But first, I need more coffee. Mama, I've got some marketing tasks to get done for you, so do you mind if I work in here for the rest of the morning?"

"Of course not."

"As for me, I'm going to go dig through the Sanctuary's basement for some interesting old thing the historic society can auction off." Damien brushed his hands down the front of his black button-down shirt. "I'm going to be covered in dust by lunchtime."

I walked Damien out, seeing him off before I headed back to my apartment to grab my laptop. It was really an old laptop of Mama's that she had loaned me for the job, and it was like hauling around a brick compared to modern versions. I had been broke when I arrived in Nightmare, and I'd sold off most of my things to get the money to buy a clunker of a car I could drive from Nashville to San Diego.

My car hadn't made it that far, but I was perfectly happy with the place it had decided to break down. Life in Nightmare was good.

Plus, I realized, I had enough money saved up that I could probably buy myself a new, inexpensive laptop. It would be a lot more convenient, especially since Mama's was so old the battery wouldn't hold a charge anymore, so it always had to be plugged in.

The idea of buying myself a shiny new laptop gave me a bounce in my step as I headed down my stairs and back to the front office. Mama even caught me humming to myself while I worked, but she thought it was for a very different reason.

"You're picturing it, aren't you?" she asked.

I looked up from the series of social media posts I was preparing and blinked at her. "Picturing what?"

"You and Damien buying a historic building to live in. You're sitting there humming to yourself, like you're the happiest girl in Nightmare."

I laughed, but I could also feel the heat rushing to my cheeks. "Believe it or not, I'm happy because I realized I have enough money to buy myself a new laptop. Damien and I aren't at that stage in our relationship, and you know it."

"You're getting there, though," Mama said. As if to make the idea even more enticing, she added, "I'll be so happy to welcome you to our family."

I winked at Mama. "You're already family, as far as I'm concerned."

After grabbing lunch in my apartment and taking a quick nap, I got back to work midway through the afternoon. I wanted to wrap up one more thing before it was time to get ready for work at the Sanctuary that evening.

I was surprised when I walked into the motel office and saw Damien again, and I told him so. "Mama called and said Nick is bringing Lucy by after school, so she thought we could all chat with the two of them about our idea for Lucille," he explained.

Sure enough, a battered old tow truck pulled up just a few minutes later. I had met Lucy's dad when my car broke

28

down outside of Nightmare, and seeing him always made me feel good. He'd been my hero that day, and he had become a friend.

Nick's eyes were as blue as his mom's, and he turned them on me as soon as he walked in the door. "Hey, Olivia!" He reached out to hug me, then stopped and wiped his hands on his grime-stained white jumpsuit. "Ah, never mind. I've been working on an old Ford that's a bit of a mess."

Before I could respond, there was a blur of pink, and Lucy's body crashed into mine in the most violent hug I'd ever received. "Hey, Miss Olivia!" She moved on to Damien next, then Mama.

"Mama says you two want to talk about something?" Nick prompted. "I assume it's about Aunt Lucille?" He and his wife, Mia, had only recently learned about the existence of ghosts, though they were still in the dark about all the other supernatural creatures that existed.

Damien and I told Nick and Lucy about the energy spring, and the possibility of taking Lucille there. She seemed to be getting stronger as a ghost or whatever kind of non-corporeal entity she had become, and we explained that we hoped the extra energy might help her progress.

"Ooh, that sounds fun!" Lucy's mass of dark curls bounced as she pretended to swim. "Like a pool, but for ghosts!"

"You'll ask Lucille if she'd like to go, then?" I asked.

Lucy nodded. "Sure. Next time she shows up, I'll ask her. And I hope she shows up soon, because there's been trouble on the playground at school."

CHAPTER FIVE

Out of the corner of my eye, I could see the way Mama's mouth dropped open. I must have looked similar, because Nick nodded his head slowly and gave me a grave look. "Lucy was telling me about it on the drive over here."

"What do you mean there's been trouble on the playground?" I asked Lucy.

"The swings are moving by themselves, and some of the girls in my class said someone took their hand, but when they looked, they didn't see anyone."

I had figured Lucy's "trouble" was ghostly in nature, but I hadn't expected the paranormal activity on the playground to be quite so dramatic. "The Vanishing Girl you see is doing all this," I said. It was a statement, not a question.

"It's all three of them! I saw them at recess, standing in a line next to the slide."

Damien and I exchanged a look, and when he spoke, I could tell he was trying to choose his words carefully. He didn't want to say anything that might frighten a ten-year-old, but he also didn't want to say anything that might clue Nick in to the fact that there were more than just ghosts in the supernatural world. Someday, Nick, Mia, and Lucy would learn the truth, but we were trying to ease them into it.

"Lucy, like we've mentioned before, we think the ghosts of those girls were trapped somewhere for a long time," Damien began. The Vanishing Girls were three girls about Lucy's age who had gone missing after school one day in nineteen fifty-nine. No one had ever been able to learn what happened to them. "The one ghost you've been seeing on the playground somehow got out of where they were trapped, but now, all three of them are free."

Lucy planted her hands on her hips. "Yeah, they sure are. And they're causing trouble!"

"It sounds like they're trying to draw attention to themselves," Mama said. "Maybe, after all those years of not being able to communicate, they're ready to make new friends."

I wasn't sure if ghosts did that kind of thing, but it seemed to comfort Lucy, who smiled. "Okay. I'll say hi to them the next time I see them. But, hopefully, Great-aunt Lucille can help out, too."

"And we can talk about it with Vivian," Nick supplied. He and Mia had approved of our suggestion that Lucy work with the Sanctuary's psychic to help her navigate her growing abilities. "She might have some good ideas."

"I'll ask her at our next practice." Lucy nodded firmly, as if she had been conducting an important piece of business that had just concluded. "I'll ask Lucille about that energy pool, too."

Lucy strode forward, her arms reaching for Mama's waist. "Bye!"

"You're not leaving just yet," Mama said, chuckling.

"We're watching the front office for a bit while your grandma goes to a Chamber of Commerce event," Nick explained. "Your grandpa can't do it because he's helping your mom with that drywall patch at the hair salon."

"Oh, we get to run the motel! Cool!" Lucy ran behind

the check-in area and plopped down into the desk chair, completely disappearing behind the Formica countertop.

"I've got to go to the Chamber mixer, too," Damien said, giving me a sly look. "Would you like to come with me?"

"I'm so over that phase of my life," I said. When I had been a high-powered marketing executive in Nashville, I'd had to attend local business events all the time. It had never really been my thing. However, tagging along would mean more time with Damien and Mama, and meeting the quirky residents of Nightmare wasn't a bad way to spend an afternoon. I heaved the most dramatic sigh I could muster. "Okay, fine, but if that drunk accountant is there again, I'm not getting stuck in a conversation with him!"

"That accountant wound up helping you solve a murder, as I recall," Damien reminded me.

"True, but there is no murder to solve at the moment, so I don't need to make small talk in search of clues."

Damien said he would drive me to the mixer, but first, I had to dash to my apartment to change into something more appropriate for a Chamber of Commerce event. My slouchy sweater and jeans weren't going to cut it. Instead, I opted for a slightly nicer sweater in a cream color paired with navy-blue pants.

When I rejoined everyone in the motel office, Damien snickered. "Corporate Olivia returns."

I tugged on the sleeve of Damien's suit. "You're one to talk."

"I think you both look fantastic," Mama said. "Now, let's go, or everyone else will have eaten the cheesy meanies already!"

"The what?" I asked, certain I had misunderstood.

"Cheesy meanies," Lucy said in a dreamy voice. "I want one!"

"You'll see," Damien told me as he opened the door. "But Mama is right; we need to go now if we're going to get any."

"I'm driving!" Mama announced loudly. "I'll get us there in time!"

Damien tended to be a fast driver, but I knew Mama could give him a run for his money in her vintage red Mustang. Apparently, a need for speed ran in the family.

The mixer was being held at a mom-and-pop restaurant in the New Downtown. The place had a beach vibe, right down to a plastic sand bucket stuffed with napkins and flatware on each table. The walls were adorned with signs that had various beach-themed puns, and a fishing net had been attached to the ceiling. Plastic crabs and lobsters dangled precariously from it, looking like they might drop onto someone's plate at any moment.

The Oasis Bar and Grill was already bustling with other Chamber members when we arrived, and Mama expertly weaved her way through the crowd as Damien and I followed. We didn't so much as say hello to anyone until we were standing at two long tables set up at the back of the restaurant. Mama greeted a man she called Sammy, then introduced him to me as the owner of the Oasis.

Even as I was saying, "Nice to meet you," Mama was already piling a paper plate with what looked like pancakes covered in melted cheese.

"Here, try one!" Mama said, thrusting the plate in my direction.

One bite made me understand why she had been so anxious to get her hands on a cheesy meanie. The thing that looked like a pancake was actually jalapeño cornbread, and despite the spicy kick, it was delicious.

A man stepped between Mama and me. "Oh, I'm so glad I didn't miss out on these! Hi, Mama. How's motel life?"

"Still bustling," Mama said around a mouthful of cheesy meanie. "We've had a good tourist season. How's fancy-pants hotel life?"

"Can't complain." The man half turned toward me. "I don't think we've met. I'm Ellis Upton."

"Ellis is the manager of the Nightmare Grand," Mama explained.

"Olivia Kendrick," I said, shaking his hand. "I work at Nightmare Sanctuary, and I do some marketing work for Cowboy's Corral."

"Busy lady," Ellis commented. He adjusted his thick, black-framed glasses, then nodded at Damien. "I'm doing double-duty today, too. I'm representing the hotel as well as the Nightmare Historic Society. We're collecting prizes for our annual fundraising raffle." As if to prove it, he lifted a blue gift box that was topped with a tiny cowboy hat instead of a bow.

"Emmett already hit us up," Damien said. "I think I have just the thing to donate."

"Outstanding!" Ellis tucked the gift box under one arm and reached for a plate. As he began to load it with food, he said, "I should have gone into real estate. That's where the real money is. We've got a guest right now who's in town looking to become Nightmare's new tourism king. He wants to buy up places and turn them into shiny new attractions."

"I thought the appeal of Nightmare was that it's not shiny and new," I noted. I couldn't imagine the town without its faded, weather-beaten feel, which added to its Wild West authenticity.

"Well, he doesn't want to make them too shiny, I suppose." Ellis self-consciously glanced down at his black pants and periwinkle-blue shirt. "Not as fancy as himself, at any rate. I've never had a guest as highfalutin as him before."

"Thank goodness I'm not too late!" A woman appeared next to Damien. It took me a moment to realize she was the owner of Bake in the Day, because when I'd met her before, her copper curls had been hidden under a scarf. "I was worried these would all be gone. It's nice when I can enjoy someone else's baking."

"Here, Chelsea, let me fix you a plate." Ellis put his own down so he could start putting cheesy meanies onto a second one. "Do you know Damien and Olivia from Nightmare Sanctuary?"

Chelsea pointed at me. "Olivia and I just met! Nice to see you again. Hi, Damien."

"Chelsea's cinnamon rolls are the tastiest thing in Nightmare," Ellis said as he handed a plate to her.

Mama had been chatting with Sammy, the restaurant's owner, and I heard him say, "Hey, now!"

"I'm talking sweet, not savory," Ellis assured him over his shoulder.

Chelsea hefted the plate. "Thanks! I hate to eat and run, but I've got to get back to the bakery once I scarf these down and say hi to a couple of folks. I have to bake more if I'm going to be able to afford that rent hike Jack is threatening."

A man who was much taller than Chelsea stepped up behind her. He snaked a muscular arm over her shoulder to help himself to her food. "Ugh, don't ruin my appetite with talk of your landlord!" He drew out the last word while rolling his eyes.

"Sorry, Sid. I promise not to complain for the next five minutes."

"Just long enough to eat these." Sid finally seemed to notice the rest of us. "Hi, everyone. I'm Chelsea's boyfriend. I'm just giving her moral support today. And eating."

Sid and Chelsea waved at us, then moved away to chat

with other people at the mixer. I felt slightly breathless watching them go. The two of them were like a little whirlwind with their energy.

Mama laughed. "I wonder if Chelsea's rent is getting a bigger increase than the rest of Jack's tenants. Jack is her ex-husband, and I'm sure he's not happy that she's seeing someone new!"

CHAPTER SIX

"Chelsea has mentioned the new beau, but this is the first time I've met him," Ellis said. "He's very...tall."

"It can't be fun having an ex for a landlord," I noted.

"No," Mama said, frowning. "It was a nasty divorce that dragged on for ages. The only upside is that it generated a lot of sympathy for Chelsea, and she wound up getting some very dedicated customers who wanted to support her and the bakery."

"Do you think—" Damien began, but he stopped short as Chelsea bustled over to us again.

"Oh, Mama! Stop by this afternoon. I've got a new recipe I'm trying out, and I want my loyal customers to give me feedback on it. If I'm in the back working, just let my son know what you're there for. He'll be up front. The rest of you are invited, too, of course."

Chelsea turned and disappeared into the crowd.

"Let me guess," I said to Mama. "You're one of those very dedicated customers who supported Chelsea during her divorce?"

Mama waved a hand. "I was a fan of her baking long before she and Jack split up."

We eventually moved away from the food tables so we could say hello to some other attendees, but after an hour,

Damien was looking at his watch more than he was looking at the people we were talking to.

"Time to go?" I asked him.

"I know my father is being looked after, but I'm not comfortable being away from him for long periods of time." Damien's forehead creased. "He's just an egg, so I feel like I need to keep an extra-close eye on him."

"Let's collect Mama," I said, taking Damien's hand. "We can drop you off at the Sanctuary, then she and I will have to put on brave faces and do the taste-test without you."

Damien gave me a lopsided grin. "If you don't get some extra and bring it to me tonight, I'm breaking up with you."

We found Mama deep in conversation with Buck Olsen, who owned a local car dealership. She was in the middle of trying to explain that she did not, in fact, want to trade in her Mustang for a two-year-old Toyota. It didn't take much to convince her we needed to head out, though Buck did look disappointed we had interrupted his sales pitch.

Mama drove to the Sanctuary, where we dropped off Damien. As Mama began to pull away, I yawned widely. "Those kinds of events always make me sleepy."

"It's a lot of work being that polite to that many people."

I chuckled. "I'm polite to a lot of people every time I take tickets here. It's different, though, when you're listening to one person after another tell you why their business is the best in town."

"Or how the Nightmare Grand is so much fancier than Cowboy's Corral," Mama said with a sniff.

In short order, I was walking through the front door of Bake in the Day for the second time in two days. Except, on this occasion, there was no argument happening outside on the boardwalk.

Instead, there was a man in a suit standing at the glass bakery display, one manicured hand pointing to a stack of baguettes. The diamonds in his gold ring sparkled as he said, "Are they made with French flour?"

"Uh." The man behind the counter, who looked like he was somewhere in his early twenties, threw a look over his shoulder. "I think we just use regular flour."

I could only see the customer from the back, but I knew what kind of facial expression he was making based on the tone of his voice. "You don't know where your ingredients are sourced from?"

"I mean, my mom orders everything. Do you want me to go ask her?" The young man ran a hand through his unruly brown hair and threw another glance toward a door behind the counter.

"Yes. Obviously." The customer crossed his arms and turned away, giving me my first glimpse of more than his backside. His gray suit looked even more expensive than anything Emmett Kline wore, and I thought wryly that Emmett and Damien both had some competition to be Nightmare's best-dressed man. I saw more sparkles and realized there were diamonds in the man's cufflinks, too.

How much money does this guy have?

The man I assumed was Chelsea's son returned. "She says no, she uses domestic flour."

"Just the tart, then."

As the rude man left, Mama turned and stared at him with a sour expression. "So pretentious," she muttered once he was gone.

"Do you get a lot of customers like that?" I asked the young man as Mama and I stepped forward.

"That was a first," he admitted.

"You're Quinn, right? I haven't seen you since you

41

were in high school," Mama said. "Your mom told us to stop by. She's recruited us to test that new recipe."

Quinn smiled. "And you're Mama, from the motel. Mom told me you were going to stop by. Hang on a sec." He ducked down behind the counter, and when he straightened up again, he had a small ramekin in each hand. As he held them out toward Mama and me, I caught the scent of cinnamon. "It's a bread pudding recipe Mom found in her grandmother's collection," Quinn explained.

Mama and I wasted no time, grabbing forks and diving right in. The bread pudding was on a par with Chelsea's cinnamon rolls, and we gave it full approval after we'd both eaten every crumb. Quinn's smile grew wider with each word of praise, and he gladly gave me an extra to take to Damien.

"Your mom said she was worried about selling enough to keep up with the higher rent, but she has nothing to worry about," Mama said, putting her empty ramekin on top of the display case. "People are going to go wild for this. Such a shame that your dad is being a lousy landlord."

Quinn's smile disappeared instantly, and his face clouded over. "Ex-stepdad," he said in a staccato. "He isn't family."

Yikes. And I thought Baxter and Damien had a difficult relationship.

Mama's cheeks reddened, but her tone was all kindness as she said, "Ex-stepdad. It's still a shame. Your mom and this bakery deserve to be treated fairly."

"If my dad were still alive, he'd take care of Jack," Quinn muttered.

Yikes again.

"Thank you for the bread pudding," I said, anxious to change the subject. "Since we're here, I'll take two of those baguettes. My co-workers will love them, and none of them will care where the flour came from. Even our French staff member won't mind."

I didn't mention Mori couldn't eat the bread, anyway, since she was a vampire. She also hadn't lived in France for a couple hundred years, but that wasn't a good conversation piece, either.

Quinn still looked disgruntled as he took my money and handed me the baguettes, but he did, at least, thank me for the business.

When Mama and I got outside, I said, "Whoa! That was tense."

"Talk about a slip of the tongue," Mama said, shaking her head. "I should have remembered Quinn's daddy died a long time ago."

"It was an honest mistake. You said Chelsea and Jack's marriage ended badly, and it clearly had a negative impact on Quinn. Poor kid."

By the time Mama was pulling into her parking spot at the motel, though, all we could think about was that bread pudding. Delicious baked goods were a great way to drive out negative thoughts.

The baguettes never made it to the dining room at the Sanctuary, where I'd planned to slice them up and hand them around before the family meeting that night. Maida, the youngest witch, was crossing the entryway as I came inside the building, and she took one and ran off with it, promising she wouldn't keep it all to herself.

I had a sneaking suspicion she was going to share it with Felipe.

The second baguette only made it as far as Zach's office. His sensitive werewolf nose had smelled the bread when I passed his doorway on my way to say hello to Damien, and he volunteered to dole it out for me.

Damien was just coming out of his office as I stepped up to his door, and he smiled as I held out the bread pudding sample. "Perfect timing. I'm heading to the dining room to go over a couple things with Justine. Shall we?"

As we walked, I filled Damien in on the delights and drama of the trip to Bake in the Day. Damien was just starting to respond as we spotted Mori coming from the direction of the basement stairs. She had an excited look on her face, and she was moving so quickly she had to hold up the hem of her long blood-red gown to prevent her feet from tripping over it.

"He hasn't hatched yet," Damien said.

Mori's gait slowed, and she gave Damien a confused look. "I didn't figure he had."

"You look excited, so I thought you were expecting to find a baby phoenix waiting for you in the dining room."

"Oh, no. I'm excited because I'm going out for dinner later with a gentleman." Mori's eyes fluttered, and she breathed out a happy sigh. "He was so delicious last night that I want seconds."

"I didn't think you and Theo usually had seconds, as you put it," I said. Mori and Theo could both mesmerize, which meant they could drink blood from people, then erase any memory of it happening. Typically, the two vampires fed from the tourists who were always coming through Nightmare, so they didn't have to worry about tipping off any locals.

"I'm making an exception," Mori said. "You could taste his wealth. The guy probably drives a car worth more than the entire Sanctuary."

I narrowed my eyes. "Let me guess. Silver hair, tailored suit, and dark eyes that could make even the bravest person quail under their stare?"

Mori gave me a knowing look. "Ah, so you've seen him. That means you can understand why I'm so excited to dine with him again."

"Technically, you're going to dine *on* him," Damien pointed out.

"It's a good thing you can't taste personality," I told Mori. "Mama and I saw him being a total jerk at the bakery today. But, if it helps you track down your dinner date, I believe he's staying at the Nightmare Grand. The manager there mentioned a current guest is a very wealthy real estate investor, and I can only assume it was the man we saw at the bakery."

"That *is* helpful information. Thank you. It's going to be fine dining for me tonight."

When we walked into the dining room, I was surprised to see Zach had kept his word about sharing the baguette. I was not surprised when Felipe ran up to me for scratches, and I could see breadcrumbs around his snout.

I was assigned to work the front of the haunt that night, taking tickets as guests came through the front door and lined up between the velvet ropes in the entryway. It was a steady but uneventful evening, and I had a fun time chatting with the guests coming through the door.

Around ten o'clock, I looked up at the next guest in line with what I thought of as my "spooky hostess" smile. I wanted to make guests feel welcome, but I also liked getting into the spirit of things. "Welcome to Nightmare Sanctuary," I said in a vaguely threatening tone, my hand extended for the man's ticket.

I traded my spooky expression for a shocked one as I realized the man was the one from the bakery that afternoon. *Why is mister "French flour or nothing" rich guy here?* I wondered. He just didn't seem like the haunted house type. We didn't have nearly enough diamonds for his taste, I was sure.

Either the man didn't recognize me, or he simply chose not to acknowledge we had seen each other earlier in the day. He handed me his ticket without a word, then glided past me.

"Have fun," I called, staring at his back for the second time that day.

Other than that unexpected encounter, the remainder of the night was a quiet one. Once the Sanctuary closed at midnight, I shut and locked the door I had propped open, then went to the locker room where I stashed my purse each night.

I had to walk through the entryway again to reach the hallway that led to Damien's office, and I was astonished to see the rich real estate investor standing there, taking photos with his cell phone. He appeared to be getting a shot of the high ceiling, which was lit to look spooky, with an occasional flash to mimic lightning.

"Excuse me," I said politely. "We're actually closed."

"Yes, I know," the man said, wholly unconcerned. "Would you please introduce me to the owner of this place? I might be interested in making an offer on it."

CHAPTER SEVEN

It took me a moment to process what the man had just said, and I gaped at him.

This guy has a real knack for surprising me.

"The Sanctuary isn't for sale," I finally managed to say. "Even if it were, the owner isn't available at the moment."

The man gave me a pinched look. "There must be someone in charge here, and they must be available. We're talking a multimillion-dollar deal here."

"But we aren't for—"

"Take me to the person who is in charge here," the man said loudly.

"Fine," I huffed. Damien would just give the same answers, though I wondered if he could get through the conversation without his eyes glowing in anger at the man's entitled behavior. "This way."

Damien's office door was open, so I knocked on the doorframe as I led the way inside. "Damien, this gentleman would like to have a chat with you."

My face must not have looked as neutral as I thought, because Damien's body tensed slightly as he stood and came around his desk.

"Leland Porter of Porter Properties," the man said grandly. He wasn't as tall as Damien, but he puffed out his chest and raised his chin as the two shook hands.

"Damien Shackleford. What can I do for you, Leland? I hope you didn't have a bad experience at the Sanctuary tonight."

"Not at all. In fact, I'm quite impressed with what I've seen. You've done a nice job renovating this old building. Historic is a hot buzzword around here, isn't it? A place like this would be a great resort. Luxury rooms upstairs, a recreation area in that wilderness out back—"

"There's a cemetery back there," I interrupted.

"Oh, that's easy enough to deal with." Leland shot an annoyed glance in my direction. "How much do you want for this place, Mr. Shackleford?"

"The Sanctuary isn't for sale."

I had been naive to think Damien's answer would be sufficient for Leland.

"I can make you a millionaire overnight," he said, taking a step forward.

"As a matter of fact, you can't. The Sanctuary is a business, and it's home to most of our staff. It is not for sale."

When Damien glanced in my direction, I raised a hand and tapped a finger against my cheek, right below my eye. He casually slid his mirrored sunglasses out of his jacket pocket and put them on to hide the growing glow in his eyes.

Maybe I should ask Zach to kick Leland out. In addition to being the Sanctuary's accountant, Zach also headed up security.

I silently backed out of the room and headed down the hallway, but as I approached Zach's office door, I had a better idea. I dashed to the dining room and was relieved to find Mori there, talking to Fiona and Seraphina. "Mori, your dinner has been delivered," I called. "And he might need to be rescued from Damien, so please hurry."

Mori did just that, rushing right past me. As she went, she called over her shoulder, "Damien's office?"

48

"Yep."

By the time I caught up, Mori was standing just behind Leland, who was throwing out numbers. "I'll write you a check for the first half right now," he said.

Damien didn't answer. Instead, he began to rub one temple with his fingers. I thought he was weary of Leland's insistence, until I saw his head wobble slightly.

He wanted Mori to mesmerize Leland.

Mori, however, hadn't gotten the message. "Damien, are you feeling unwell? Perhaps I can take this gentleman out for a drink while you get some rest."

"Mori, if I haven't said it already, you look downright *mesmerizing* tonight," I said pointedly.

"Thank you, Olivia. That's very sweet of you."

"Yes," Damien chimed in. "It would be a shame for anyone to *forget* this moment."

Mori snickered. "Oh, is that what you've been getting at?" She turned to Leland and curled her fingers around his arm, maneuvering so she could stare into his eyes. Her gaze was intense, but her voice was a hypnotic monotone. "You and I are definitely going out for a drink. You want to go out with me, right now, and you will leave this man alone."

"Okay," Leland said. He turned to Damien. "Good night. I'm taking her out for a drink."

"Good night," Damien said, looking like he was going to start laughing.

Once Mori and her jerk of a dinner had left, Damien plopped down into his desk chair and made a noise that was half-groan, half-laugh. "That guy was something else."

"He's the guy Mama and I saw being so rude at the bakery earlier."

"Leland says he's buying up historic properties in Southwestern tourist towns, and he wants to get a handful here in Nightmare. He told me the trick is to get grants to restore historic places, then charge tourists an arm and a leg to come stay in the old buildings."

"I'm all for historic preservation, but it sounds like he's in it for the money."

"Yeah." Damien's voice was distant. He was quiet for a moment, then he stood. "Come on. Let's go have a chat with the others."

Zach was just coming out of his office as we passed his door. "Meeting in the dining room," Damien told him. "Spread the word."

Clara and Fiona were in the entryway, and Damien said the same to them.

Before long, nearly everyone had gathered in the dining room. Damien had finally taken off his sunglasses, though I noticed his eyes still had a dull green glow to them. Leland Porter had really gotten under his skin.

Instead of stepping up to the podium, Damien stood in front of it, raising his voice so everyone could hear him clearly. "The Sanctuary is not for sale," he said firmly.

There was a ripple of murmuring, and Damien continued, "Someone tonight made a very aggressive offer for this place, and I assured him we aren't going anywhere. If any of you are asked, by this man or anyone else, you can assure them the Sanctuary is our home, and we are not interested in selling it."

"We believe you," Seraphina said. She was curled up in the barrel-sized water tank on wheels that allowed her to move from one place to another. "But if you already told this guy no, then what makes you think he'll ask any of us?"

"Like I said, it was an aggressive offer." Damien hesitated. "I don't think he's done, and he said some things tonight that gave me the impression he would be looking for any loopholes that might help him get his hands on this place. He threw out some legal terms I don't even know, but there was a threat in the way he said them."

"But this is our home," Fiona said. She gestured toward Seraphina. "Where would we go if we couldn't live here?" As a banshee, Fiona could pass as a normal human. People would simply think she was eccentric with her pale skin and long, flowing black hair. Seraphina, though, would never know what it was like to walk around on two legs, or to live outside of the water.

"I don't care to go back to a ruined castle in Europe," Gunnar declared. His wings extended slightly as he swept his clawed hands around the room. "These are my people. Besides, I've gotten spoiled by electricity and air-conditioning."

"Where do other gargoyles live?" I asked. Gunnar's massive size was enough to make him stand out in a crowd. Add in his sinewy wings and his skin tone—which was gray with a light-green, moss-like covering—and he would never be able to settle into a normal neighborhood.

Not to mention the fact that he never bothered to wear clothes.

"Like I said, ruined castles. Here in the states, gargoyles usually stick to caves, though I've got a few contacts who took up residence in a ghost town in a remote region of Colorado." Gunnar's expression was self-satisfied as he said, "They don't have air-conditioning, like we do."

"We're safe," Damien reiterated. "But I don't want to give Leland Porter any foot in the door here. Again, if he comes around, tell him to shop elsewhere."

Damien had delivered his message, so some people wandered out while others broke into small groups, their heads close together and their expressions worried.

"This isn't what I was trying to accomplish." Damien's mouth was close to my ear, so only I would hear it.

I slid an arm around his waist. "I know. But it's good

for everyone to be aware of what's happening, in case they hear any rumors about someone sniffing around the Sanctuary. And even though they're worried in the moment, it never hurts for you to reassure them their home and livelihood aren't going anywhere."

"That guy really got to me. Between my dad being an egg and my mother being a ghost because she wanted to protect me, I'm already on edge. Leland showing up was more than I could take."

I was trying to comfort Damien, but at the same time, I had to laugh at the picture he had just painted of his parents. "We are quite the motley crew," I told him.

Damien and I both stayed later than usual, and by the time I left the Sanctuary around two o'clock in the morning, my co-workers had all relaxed, and the mood was much lighter than it had been during Damien's announcement. Like I had told Damien, everyone had processed the news and realized there was no point in hand-wringing.

I woke up later than usual on Friday morning, and I had just finished putting on a floral dress and blue cardigan when my phone rang. A glance at the caller ID showed me it was Mama.

"Hey, Mama," I answered.

My tone had been perky, but Mama's was subdued. "Olivia, I need you in the office, please."

"I'll be right there," I said, already heading toward my door. I didn't know why she needed me, but I could tell something was wrong.

I got a sinking feeling when I got close to the office and saw a Nightmare Police Department cruiser parked out front. I yanked on the door and ran inside, and Luis Reyes turned to me with a startled expression.

"Officer Rey...Luis!" I was still getting used to calling him by his first name. We had agreed to be on a first-name basis months earlier, but since he had started dating Justine,

I was making even more of an effort. "Mama? What's going on?"

"Since you and I were at the bakery yesterday, Luis wants to ask us some questions."

I pressed a hand to my forehead and groaned. "Leland Porter was murdered last night, wasn't he?"

"Who?" Reyes and Mama asked at the same time.

I dropped my hand and looked between the two of them. "Clearly, my guess is incorrect."

"You're wrong about the person but correct about a murder." Reyes ran a hand through his dark hair. "Jack Wiley was killed inside the bakery this morning."

CHAPTER EIGHT

"Oh, the landlord was murdered," I said. "That makes a lot more sense."

Mama gave me a horrified look. "A man was murdered in Chelsea's bakery!"

"It's awful," I agreed. "But given everything we've been hearing the past couple days about Jack, it's easier to understand that someone went after him rather than Leland."

"Again with this Leland guy," Reyes said. He already had his small notebook in his hands. "Is he a suspect we need to speak to?"

"A man," Mama said again, enunciating each word, "was murdered in Chelsea's bakery."

"Yes, I… Oh. I understand, Mama. You're worried Chelsea is a suspect." My head swiveled between Mama and Reyes as I looked for confirmation.

"I'm not here to share details of the case," Reyes said. "I want to know what happened when the two of you visited the bakery yesterday."

"How was he killed?" I asked.

Reyes made a noise of exasperation, and he gave me a look that said he must be the most patient man in the world. "Ms. Kendrick, please."

Uh-oh. He's using my last name.

"Leland was in there when we walked in," I said, giving Reyes exactly what he was asking for before he could get any more frustrated with me. "He was an absolute jerk to Chelsea's son, who was working up front."

"Quinn," Mama supplied. "He had more patience with that entitled snob than I would have. By the way, Olivia, how do you know the rude man's name?"

"He and I met last night, when he lingered after-hours at the Sanctuary so he could pester Damien about buying the place."

Reyes was writing furiously in his notebook. "Hmm. What else?"

"Actually," Mama said, so quietly I could barely hear her, "Quinn did get mad, but it wasn't with Leland." She hesitantly recounted Quinn's reaction when she had mistakenly referred to Jack as his dad.

"Hmm," Reyes said again.

"He's a nice boy," Mama said in a louder voice. "I'm not suggesting he had anything to do with the murder, and I hate having to tell you what happened with him."

Reyes finally looked up from his notebook, and he fixed his reddish-brown eyes on Mama's face. "You did the right thing by telling me the truth."

"I know." Mama laced her hands together tightly. "I just don't want to get that young man in trouble."

"I was heading to the bakery on Thursday, and I over-heard Jack and the manager of the general store having an argument," I said. "It was about Jack's plan to raise the rent."

"Fred and Jack being at odds with each other isn't new," Reyes said.

"Still, perhaps you should go talk to Fred, too."

Reyes snorted out a laugh. "Thank you for telling me how to do my job." He looked at me, then Mama. "By the way, this was a normal murder, in case you were wondering."

Mama and I both nodded our understanding. Reyes had only recently found out about the supernatural world, after seeing a few ghouls drop dead. It had been a difficult conversation between Justine and him, but the two of them had come out of it still dating each other. Plus, Justine said Reyes thought her telekinetic abilities were kind of cool.

"How did he die, if it was normal?" I asked. *It can't hurt to try again.*

To my surprise, my second attempt worked.

"Head injury," Reyes said.

"Don't feel bad about telling us." Mama patted Reyes on the arm. "We would have known everything by lunchtime, anyway. I would have just called folks I know who are plugged into Nightmare's gossip."

"Someone hit Jack over the head with a blunt object, hard enough to kill him." Reyes raised a hand as I opened my mouth to ask another question. "No, we do not know what the object was. It would appear the killer didn't leave it behind, though Chelsea and Quinn both said nothing seems to be missing from the bakery."

Reyes wasn't willing to tell us any more than that, or perhaps, it was all he did know at the moment. Either way, he wouldn't answer any of the other questions Mama and I asked. We gave up trying when Reyes mentioned he had to get back to the station.

Once it was just Mama and me in the office, she slapped a palm on the Formica countertop. "This is unbelievable! How dare he suspect Chelsea of murder?"

"Luis didn't say that at all," I reminded her.

"Doesn't matter. I could tell. Since Jack was killed in the bakery, Luis has her on the suspect list."

I didn't argue. Mama might have refused to embrace her psychic abilities, but when she got what she called vibes about a person, I knew better than to question her instincts.

I shook my head. "Poor Chelsea. And poor Jack! He might have been a jerk, but no one deserves to get murdered. I hope it's all sorted out soon."

"We're going to see Chelsea, right now." Mama picked up her cell phone. "Benny's working on a leak in room five, but I'll tell him to come mind the office for a bit."

I reached a hand toward Mama. "Chelsea is probably under a lot of stress right now," I cautioned. "She might need some breathing room."

"What she needs is help. I'm giving her something better than breathing room. I'm giving her Nightmare's best amateur sleuth! You're coming with me."

"Oh. I... Well, that's... Um." I felt both flattered and dismayed, but there was no way Mama was going to let me say no. In less than ten minutes, I was in the passenger seat of her Mustang, still trying to form a coherent sentence as she sped down the two-lane road that served as Nightmare's main thoroughfare.

Chelsea's house was a cute little place, with adobe walls and a red tile roof. The yard was sparsely populated with a prickly-pear cactus and a few low bushes with pink and yellow flowers, but there were dozens of stained-glass butterflies hanging from metal spikes driven into the ground. In the midday sun, they shone beautifully, throwing patches of bright colors all over the bare dirt yard.

Despite my warning to Mama that Chelsea might not want visitors, Chelsea smiled wanly when she opened the door and stepped out to wrap her arms around Mama. "Thank goodness you're here," Chelsea said. "Come on in."

Chelsea ushered us into a living room with a shabby but comfortable couch and framed photos of butterflies.

At least I don't have to ask Chelsea what her favorite animal is.

"Do you want something to drink? A scone?" Chelsea asked.

"No, dear, we're fine," Mama assured her. "We came here to check on you."

Chelsea nodded once, then slowly eased into a chair opposite the couch, where Mama and I had settled. "The whole thing is surreal. Jack and I disliked each other so much, but I never wanted to see him dead."

"Did you find him?" I asked.

"Yeah. I always get to the bakery really early, so I can get the first batches of the day going before we open up. I usually come in through the front door, and I just leave it unlocked while I'm back in the kitchen." Chelsea shrugged. "It's Nightmare, you know? It's safe here. Or, I thought it was. Besides, half the time, I'm so busy baking that I sail right past opening time without realizing it. It's a lot easier to hear a customer ringing the bell on the counter than to hear someone knocking on the door."

"Jack came in, but you didn't hear him," Mama guessed.

"Exactly. I heard a weird noise, like something had fallen over, but I was in the middle of kneading dough, so I got that wrapped up before I went to see what had happened. There was Jack, sprawled out in the middle of the floor." Chelsea looked at her hands. "If I had gone to check it out as soon as I heard the noise, I might have seen who clobbered him."

"If you had, you might have gotten clobbered, too," Mama said.

"What am I going to do? I can't make any money while my bakery is a crime scene." Chelsea flopped back into the chair and stared at the ceiling. "And who do I even pay my rent checks to? Rumor has it some rich guy from Phoenix is looking to buy old buildings around Nightmare. What if

59

he buys my place and hikes up the rent even more than Jack was going to?"

I thought back to the interaction between Leland and Quinn at the bakery. Had Leland been there to scope the place out, even before the landlord had been murdered? Maybe he had bought the tart to see if he even wanted to have the bakery as a rental property.

"And what about Quinn?" Chelsea's voice was rising in pitch and volume. *She could have a second career as a banshee,* I thought. "He already had to go through my awful divorce, and now a murder investigation? He just wants some peace and quiet. My poor boy."

Mama and I exchanged a surreptitious glance. Neither one of us was going to tell Chelsea her son was possibly a suspect in Jack's murder. Quinn might be a nice guy most of the time, but he had even said if his dad had still been alive, he would have "taken care of" Jack. Had Quinn taken matters into his own hands?

Chelsea choked back a sob.

"Olivia can help," Mama said, leaning forward and touching a hand to Chelsea's knee.

I shifted uncomfortably and self-consciously smoothed out my dress. "I'll try. I can ask around to see what people know, and maybe I can get some intel on the real estate buyer. I've met Leland, so that shouldn't be hard."

"Thank you," Chelsea said with a sniff.

I was silent after Mama and I said our goodbyes, and it wasn't until we had driven a couple of miles that Mama asked, "What's going on in your head, Olivia?"

"I truly believe Chelsea didn't kill Jack, but I don't think we can rule out Quinn."

"I agree. Who else is a suspect, though? Fred Corcoran, for sure. We can stop by the general store and have a chat with him."

I smiled at Mama. "Who's the amateur sleuth now?"

"I'm just trying to help a friend. Besides, it's a nice day for a stroll down High Noon Boulevard."

Except, when Mama parked near the heart of Nightmare's tourism, I realized the general store wasn't her real goal. "We're not here to talk to Fred or to take a stroll," I said after we had climbed out of the car. "You parked close to the bakery, because you want to see the crime scene for yourself!"

Mama made a face of mock innocence.

We cut over to High Noon Boulevard, and we stepped up onto the boardwalk in time to see Fred walking out of the saloon. Since he was wearing a Western shirt, jeans, and cowboy boots, Fred looked picture-perfect as he strode through the swinging half-doors.

Leland Porter, who was on Fred's heels, stuck out like a sore thumb. His tailored navy-blue suit didn't fit the saloon's Wild West vibe at all.

It's just a coincidence they're leaving the saloon at the same time.

Except it wasn't. As Mama and I watched, Fred turned and shook hands with Leland. They exchanged a few words, and then Leland gave Fred a friendly smack on the shoulder before the two turned and walked off in different directions.

CHAPTER NINE

"What was that about?" I asked.

"Isn't that the guy we saw in the bakery yesterday?" Mama didn't need my confirmation, because she was already pursing her lips and staring at Leland as he crossed the street. "What are he and Fred up to?"

"Fred rents the space the general store is in," I noted. "If Leland wants to buy the place, he should be talking to Jack, the landlord."

"Except Jack was murdered this morning."

"Right."

"Maybe Leland wants to know if it's worth being the landlord of the general store," Mama speculated. "You know, will Fred keep the place up and running for a long time to come, does it make enough income that Leland can charge what he wants for rent, and that sort of thing."

"I wondered the same with Leland's visit to the bakery. Maybe he was scoping the place out." I laughed sardonically. "Of course! I thought it was strange when he came through the line for the Sanctuary last night, because he doesn't seem like the kind of man who would enjoy a haunted house attraction. But if he was there to see how good business is, or to check out the building itself... Do you know he proposed turning the Sanctuary into an expensive resort?"

Mama rolled her eyes. "I don't like him, and I haven't even met him yet."

"I have a feeling Jack's murder isn't going to be as simple to solve as we'd hoped."

"You know what will help you feel better? A beer. Let's pop into the saloon."

I glanced at my watch. "It's only lunchtime."

Mama waved a hand airily. "It's for a good cause."

That cause, I knew, wasn't about making me feel better. It was about getting clues. Mama was already heading for the swinging doors, and I smiled as I followed.

The saloon wasn't crowded, and we slid up onto two empty stools along the bar that ran across the back wall. The brass fittings and big antique mirror were original to the bar, and it was fun to think of all the copper miners and cowboys who had stared at their own reflections in that same mirror during the past century and a half.

No sooner had our bartender, dressed as a can-can dancer, put two mugs of beer in front of us than Mama went in for the clues. "You know Fred, the manager over at the general store, right? I just saw him coming out of here with some rich-looking guy."

The bartender nodded her chin toward a spot to my left. "Yeah, the two of them were sitting at a table over in the corner. Fred had a beer, but the other guy drank the most expensive whiskey we have. Terrible tipper, though."

"Were they having a meeting?"

"Whatever they were talking about, there was a lot of back-slapping and clinking of glasses. You'd think they were celebrating, the way they were acting."

"I wonder what they were celebrating," I said.

The bartender gave a little shrug, clearly uninterested in knowing. As she moved down the line to help a couple who had sat down a few stools away from us, Mama leaned toward me and whispered, "Were they toasting to Jack's demise?"

"Maybe. But, if they were, were they also toasting to their own success in bringing it about? Both of them were already on my suspect list. Maybe they're working together."

I swiveled on my barstool so I could look at the area the bartender had indicated when she said Fred and Leland had been sitting at a table. There was a vacant one sitting in the corner, with a beer mug and a whiskey glass sitting on it. Unfortunately, the tables nearby weren't occupied, either, which meant we wouldn't be able to ask if anyone had overheard the discussion.

I turned back to the bar and raised my glass to Mama. "You were right. This beer is making me feel better. Fred and Leland are looking a lot more like suspects than Quinn or Chelsea."

Mama clinked her glass against mine. "Yes, they are."

Since Benny had things under control at the motel, Mama suggested we stop by the Sanctuary after our trip to the saloon so she could check on Baxter. Of course, before that, we had to walk past the bakery. There wasn't anything to see, though, except yellow crime scene tape strung up in front of the door. The police appeared to have wrapped up their investigation inside, because the lights were off, and all we could spot was a sad pile of unsold rolls sitting in a basket on top of the display case.

When I reminded Mama that our original intent in visiting High Noon Boulevard had been to chat with Fred, she instantly nixed the idea of going to see him. "Not after what we learned in the saloon," she insisted. "I'd be too nervous about dropping a hint that we know he and Leland are up to something, and I'd ruin the whole thing."

I readily agreed because I had the same worry. Besides,

going to the Sanctuary meant I'd get to see Damien while Mama visited with the egg that was her brother-in-law.

My life in Nashville had been so boring compared to life in Nightmare.

We found both Damien and Baxter in Damien's office. The birdcage was sitting on the hearth, and Damien had a small blaze going in the fireplace. It made the office stiflingly warm, but he said Seraphina had told him to do it. "She said my father's notes mention warming the egg as a way of encouraging hatching," he explained.

"Did you hear about the murder?" Mama asked Damien as she touched the birdcage. In a softer voice, she said, "Hey, there, Baxter."

Damien looked up from the pile of papers on his desk. "Murder? Anyone we know?"

"No. Someone killed the landlord who owns the bakery and the general store locations," I said. "Jack…"

"Wiley," Mama supplied.

"Right. Jack Wiley got his head bashed in at the bakery."

I heard footsteps behind me, and I turned to see Malcolm and Zach coming into the office. Zach settled for giving us all a gruff nod, but Malcolm swept his black top-hat off his bald head and bowed deeply. "Ladies," he said. He bent down to kiss the top of Mama's fluffy hair. "What a nice surprise."

"What's this about a head getting bashed in?" Zach asked.

"There was a murder early this morning," I said. Mama and I quickly gave a rundown of what had happened at the bakery, followed by an account of our visit to Chelsea's house and the saloon.

I was surprised when all three men began to snicker. "This is a serious matter," I said.

"It is," Malcolm agreed, straining to keep a straight face. "It's the idea of you and Mama running around Nightmare like a couple of private investigators that has me smiling."

"The motel P-Is," Zach suggested. "The Cowboy's Corral Crime Fighters."

"Oh, enough," Mama said, though she was smiling, too. "Chelsea has been a friend for a long time, and you can't blame me for wanting to help her out."

"Speaking of helping someone out," Damien said, "would you two like to make a delivery for me while you're out searching for suspects? I found a good piece to donate for the historic society's raffle."

"You're not donating us, are you?" Tanner had just emerged from the bookcase next to the fireplace.

"Of course not," Damien said.

"Good. Me and McCrory would have a thing or two to say if you tried to get rid of us." Tanner looked at the bird-cage. "I just came to see if the egg was hatching yet. I'll go tell McCrory we've got to keep waiting."

As Tanner disappeared back through the bookcase, Justine and Clara came into the room, squeezing past Zach.

"No one told us there was a party in here," Clara said in her high voice.

"We're actually just heading out," Mama said. "But, Damien, I need to get back to the motel because Benny's got to head to a doctor's appointment soon. So your delivery will have to wait."

"All right. Emmett told me to take it to Ellis over at the Nightmare Grand, so I'll run it by later."

"I'll take it for you," Justine piped up.

"I'm going, too!" Clara turned her violet eyes on Damien. "What, exactly, are we taking there?"

"An old medical model of a skull," Damien answered.

"And why in the world are you two so quick to volunteer for the job?" I asked.

Clara waved an arm. "It's the Grand."

At my blank stare, she continued. "You haven't been in there, have you? Oh, you're coming with us."

"We'll have afternoon tea there," Justine suggested. "The prop repairs in the hospital vignette can wait."

"First beer, and now tea," I mumbled.

There was noise from the hallway, and we all turned to see who else was going to squeeze into Damien's already-crowded office. Instead of a person, though, it was Felipe.

"You are not invited to tea," Justine told him as he looked up at her with wide eyes.

"I've got something better than scones and tiny sandwiches," Malcolm said. "Come on, Felipe. You want some bacon scraps?"

As Malcolm and Felipe disappeared, I moved over to Damien and gave him a kiss. Behind me, Justine and Clara *ooh*ed.

"How long are you two going to tease us?" I asked as I turned to them. I tried to give them a disapproving look, but my smile totally ruined it.

Justine grinned. "At least until the end of the year."

"But it's only March!" Damien and I protested in unison.

"That's right!" Clara said happily.

Damien handed over the skull that he'd stashed in a desk drawer, and I headed out with Justine and Clara. As Justine drove us to the Nightmare Grand, I filled the two of them in on the murder. Unlike the smiles Mama and I had gotten from the men, Justine and Clara quickly offered to help however they could.

"First, though," Justine said, "tea! I can't believe you've never been to the Grand, Olivia."

"I've been past it plenty of times, but I never had a reason to go in." The old hotel had been around since Nightmare's time as a bustling copper mining town in the latter half of the nineteenth century, and it had been carefully restored to its former glory. All I knew about the inside of the place was that rooms were a lot more expensive than they were at Cowboy's Corral.

The Nightmare Grand was one street over from High Noon Boulevard, and it had an impressive facade. The red bricks had probably arrived by train, and at three stories tall, the hotel towered over the smaller buildings next to it. Big windows on the ground floor offered a view of an elegant wooden check-in desk and a seating area filled with red velvet chairs.

As soon as I took my first step into the hotel, I knew why Justine and Clara had been so excited to visit. The view from the outside didn't do the place justice. The high ceiling was covered in molded flowers and swirls, all centered around a crystal chandelier that glittered in the sunlight. Straight ahead, a double staircase curved up to the second floor, the carved railing gleaming with polish. The walls were adorned with paintings depicting Nightmare landmarks.

"Wow." I stopped to take in the details, then waved the model skull in the air. "I guess we should find Ellis first, so I can give him this thing."

Justine began to lead us to the right, toward a nondescript door she said likely led to the hotel's offices. The hallway behind the door was equally uninteresting, with a plain, worn cream carpet and not a single piece of art on the walls.

"Definitely the administrative area," Clara said. "So boring."

As we walked down the hall, we suddenly heard boisterous laughter, and a man said gleefully, "He got exactly what he deserved!"

A moment later, Ellis Upton walked out of a door directly ahead of us.

CHAPTER TEN

Ellis stopped short and stared at the three of us. His face paled, and his eyes took on a panicked expression. "This area is staff-only," he said.

"Who got what they deserved?" I asked.

Ellis opened his mouth, closed it, then opened it again. "I was just... That was a private phone conversation..." Ellis raised his eyes to the ceiling and shrugged. "Oh, why try to hide it? I didn't like Jack Wiley, and I'm not surprised someone finally got fed up enough to take him out. He was always trying to get around the historic district rules, making my life as head of the historic society an absolute nightmare."

"A nightmare in Nightmare," Justine quipped. "Sorry, I know murder isn't something to joke about."

"I'm the one who you just caught laughing about it, remember?" Ellis shook his head. He looked chagrined about being caught, but he didn't seem to feel remorse for his feelings.

"If you're not surprised Jack was killed," I asked, "then do you have an idea who might have done it?"

Ellis gave me a rueful smile. "In other words, is there anyone who looks more guilty than I do right now? I certainly don't think Chelsea Gentry killed him, despite their history. I wouldn't put it past her new boyfriend, though."

"Sid, right? I met him yesterday at the Chamber event, but I didn't talk to him much."

"I've heard him and Jack get into it a couple of times. He never approved of the way Jack treated Chelsea, both as a husband and a landlord."

"It's one thing to stand up for your girlfriend, and another to kill for her," Justine said. I was sure she was thinking of Reyes, who had recently stood up for her and the rest of us at the Sanctuary.

"You're right, but Sid had a temper. Ask that long-haired guy you work with about him."

"The redhead? Always grumpy?" I asked.

"Redhead?" Ellis narrowed his eyes. "No, brown hair. Always has a look on his face like he wants to cause a little mischief."

"Theo," I said as Justine and Clara nodded.

"I don't remember the details, because it was ages ago. But after a very long night at the saloon, Sid and Theo got into it. Maybe your friend will remember what happened."

It might have been a long night at the saloon for Sid, but I figured Theo had been there to search for someone to feed from. Catching tourists leaving the saloon was an easy way for both him and Mori to "get dinner," as they liked to put it.

"We'll ask him about it just as soon as he gets—"

"Back from the store," Justine interrupted me.

"Um, exactly. Anyway, Ellis, we came back here to give you this. It's from the days when our place was the Nightmare Sanctuary Hospital and Asylum. And don't worry, it's not a real skull but a medical model."

"Oh, thank you," Ellis said, gratefully taking the skull. He gingerly set it on a side table between an ornate but tarnished brass lamp and a basket filled with coffee and mugs. "Old pieces like this always get a lot of high bids. Tell Damien the historic society appreciates the donation."

"Now that our work here is done," Clara said brightly, "it's time for tea."

We said goodbye to Ellis and retraced our steps. Justine and Clara knew the way to the tearoom, and as we approached the wide entryway that led into it, I leaned close to Justine. "Thanks for saving me back there."

"It wouldn't have been a big deal if you'd said we'd talk to Theo as soon as he got up," Justine told me. "I just sort of panicked. Luis realized Theo was a vampire because of the fact that he only ever shows up after dark, so I figured there was no need to let anyone else know the guy sleeps all day."

"And how did Luis feel about Theo being an undead creature?" I asked.

"He told me it's Fiona who weirds him out the most." Justine laughed. "He doesn't like the idea of a banshee showing up to tell him he's going to die soon."

"That's an easy problem to solve," Clara said. "Luis just has to not die."

"This place really is grand," I noted as we entered the tearoom. The floral wallpaper had deep-red flocked velvet on it, and the dark trim gave the place a feel of coziness and wealth. About two-thirds of the tables were already occupied, and the tall trays in the center of each table had an array of petit fours, scones, and fruit on them.

A young woman with a long braid and a simple green dress ushered us to a table. Soon, I was sinking my teeth into an apricot scone smothered with clotted cream.

"Do you think this Sid guy would really murder just because he didn't want his girlfriend's rent to go up?" Justine asked. She had a half-eaten watercress sandwich in her hand, and she was looking at it thoughtfully. "I love that bakery, but I wouldn't kill for it."

I brushed a few crumbs off my fingers. "Ellis did say Sid has a temper. And if Jack was a jealous ex, it's possible the two of them got into a fight over Chelsea."

"Don't discount Fred Corcoran," Clara said as she dumped two heaping tablespoons of sugar into her teacup. *Fairies must have resilient teeth or very good dentists,* I thought. "He's been the owner of the general store for ages, and he's not the kind of guy to back down from a challenge. He stands up for himself, and he stands up for his store."

"But would he kill for his store?" Justine pressed. "That's what it all comes down to, right? These suspects might be tough people who will fight things like rent hikes, but who would go so far as to murder someone?"

"Maybe a rich real estate guy would kill to get a piece of historic property," I said under my breath. "Leland Porter just walked in."

Justine sat up a little straighter. "Oh, the guy who offered to buy the Sanctuary? Which one is he? Oh, never mind. It has to be that stuck-up-looking man in the black suit. I thought Emmett Kline was the only person in Nightmare fancy enough to wear cufflinks."

I had hoped Leland would sit down at a table on the opposite side of the room, sparing me from having to say hello. Instead, he spotted me and walked right over to our table. "We meet again," he said, reaching out to shake my hand. "And who are your lovely companions?"

Clara's nose wrinkled at that, but she smiled politely at Leland when I introduced her and Justine. "They both live and work at the Sanctuary," I added pointedly.

"Speaking of Nightmare Sanctuary," Leland said, "I can't quite remember where we left things Thursday night. I'm sure Mr. Shackleford was on the verge of accepting my offer to buy the place."

I put down my teacup and clamped my hands together in my lap. It was taking every ounce of willpower I had not to laugh. Mori had, apparently, mesmerized Leland a little too well that evening.

"The Sanctuary is not for sale," Clara said dutifully.

"She's right," I told Leland. "Damien has no interest in selling. But I'm sure you've got your eye on some other wonderful historic properties around Nightmare."

"A few, but there's nothing like that old hospital."

"Isn't Bake in the Day in an old building?" Justine asked, as if she didn't already know the answer. "Oh, that bakery makes the most divine eclairs. You should buy that place, but make Chelsea pay her rent in baked goods."

Leland gave Justine a patient smile, like she was a sweet, clueless child. "My accountant would disapprove of that, my dear. And I think the bakery could use a few improvements." Leland looked around, then sniffed disapprovingly. "Well, I came in here, thinking I would get a late lunch, but a scone isn't going to be nearly enough for me. I'm off to find something more filling before I go inspect another piece of property."

"Another potential hotel?" I asked.

"No. The upstairs of this place would be a winter home for me. Downstairs? Who knows. Maybe a retail shop. Perhaps a day spa. The tourists could use a little pampering." Leland wandered off, talking to himself about saunas and staying hydrated in the desert.

"No wonder Damien was in such a mood after their meeting," Clara said. "All the money in the world can't buy you a personality."

"Or the ability to read the room," I said. "I think Leland Porter is a man who's used to getting his way, and he pushes back until he gets it."

"A better-dressed version of Fred Corcoran, then," Clara said. She aggressively bit into a cucumber sandwich.

"And since Leland and Fred were together at the saloon earlier, appearing to be in a celebratory mood, it makes you wonder." I picked up my teacup. "But, at the moment, the only clues I want to look for are right here on this table."

"Yes, I'm interrogating the sandwich," Clara said. To prove it, she popped the final bite into her mouth.

"I'll question the jam," Justine offered.

We were finishing off the last of our food when the hostess came over to our table. She looked in the direction of the entryway, then leaned down. "I heard the three of you discussing the murder." She looked at me. "You're the woman who helped clear Ella's name."

I nodded. My friend and usual server at The Lusty Lunch Counter had been accused of murdering the diner's new dishwasher, and I tracked down the real killer.

"Please," the hostess said, her brown eyes wide, "you need to look into Ellis. He's a good boss, but I'm afraid he might have had something to do with that landlord getting killed."

"I know Ellis said Jack got what he deserved," I told her in a reassuring tone, "but it takes a lot more than that to make someone a suspect."

The hostess shook her head. "It's way worse than that. He and Fred Corcoran were threatening Jack."

CHAPTER ELEVEN

The hostess looked nervously toward the doorway again, her braid whipping over her shoulder as she did so.

"I did hear Fred and Jack arguing," I said, keeping my voice as low as hers, "but what makes you think Fred and Ellis were threatening Jack?"

"Not here. Tonight? I can pretend I'm meeting friends at your haunted house."

"What's your name?" Justine asked.

"Rose."

"Rose, I'm Justine. I'm the manager of the Sanctuary. Come by at six forty, and we'll meet you at the front door."

Rose straightened up. "Okay." She hurried away from our table, still throwing glances around the room.

As much as I wanted to discuss what Rose had said right then and there, I knew I would have to wait until we had left. Justine and Clara seemed as eager to dive into the information as I was, because the three of us hastily swallowed the last of our tea, and Clara flagged down our server for the check.

As soon as we were back in Justine's car, the three of us began talking at once. It was Justine whose voice finally won the battle. "Did Rose mean that Fred and Ellis were teaming up to threaten Jack? Or were they doing it separately?"

"And why would they be doing it, anyway?" Clara wondered. "Just because Jack was a lousy landlord?"

"There has to be more to it," I said. "What a bizarre plot twist."

"I'm anxious to know what we'll learn from Rose tonight," Justine said as she guided the car onto the street. "In the meantime, I'm sure I'll make up a thousand different wild scenarios. Olivia, where am I taking you?"

"Home, please. I want to fill Mama in, and I need to start a load of laundry."

Even though we knew speculation was fruitless, it didn't stop us from doing it as we made the short trip from the Nightmare Grand to Cowboy's Corral. Once we arrived, I hurried into the office, then had to stand and wait while Mama finished checking in a family of four.

"Finally!" I said as soon as the new guests had left. "Mama, I have to tell you what happened at the Grand!"

"I don't know what this woman witnessed," Mama said when I had finished, "but I don't think either Ellis or Fred would bully someone. Well, Fred, maybe. But not Ellis. He's more likely to bore someone to death with a detailed history of Nightmare than to bludgeon someone with a blunt object."

"The two of them don't give off killer vibes?" I asked.

"I'm not taking anyone off the suspect list," Mama assured me. "And I'm as eager as you to know what you're going to learn tonight. I expect you to march right up here tomorrow morning to give me the scoop!"

I promised I would, then headed back to my apartment to gather up my laundry.

I arrived at the Sanctuary shortly before sundown, ready to pounce on Theo as soon as he emerged from the basement. Since I had a bit of extra time, though, I said hello to Damien first. Not surprisingly, Justine and Clara had already given him a full report.

"Justine says she's just happy there wasn't a dead body underneath the table at tea," Damien told me.

"That's fair." Justine was a fan of saying she only ran across bodies when she was with me. "Do you want to come with me to interrogate Theo?"

"He's going to be thrilled that he gets to be part of an investigation, you know." Before we could do that, though, Damien grabbed the birdcage and walked it to the dining room. Fiona and Seraphina were already there, chatting with Gunnar, and the three of them happily agreed to keep an eye on Baxter.

The basement wasn't a place I had visited often. One half was used for storage, while the other had been converted into windowless apartments for vampires. There was no doubt which one was Theo's, thanks to the skull-and-crossbones pirate flag he'd hung on the wall next to his door.

Damien knocked, and Theo answered a few seconds later, still buttoning his billowing white pirate shirt. He hadn't brushed his hair yet, and it hung wildly around his shoulders.

"What happened?" Theo asked as soon as he saw our faces.

"Nothing," I assured him.

"And by nothing," Damien hurried to add, "Olivia means there's been a murder, but the person had nothing to do with anyone here at the Sanctuary."

"Right," I agreed. "However, one of the suspects does have a history with you."

Theo's eyes widened, and he stepped back. "Come on in. Who do I know that might be a murderer?"

"A guy named Sid. He's currently dating Chelsea Gentry, who owns Bake in the Day. Jack Wiley, her landlord and ex-husband, was found dead in the bakery this morning."

"Sid," Theo said slowly. "It's not ringing a bell."

"Tall guy," I supplied. "Lots of muscles. Ellis Upton over at the Nightmare Grand said you and Sid got into it one night at the saloon."

"Ellis?" Theo still looked confused. He stared down at the ground for a moment, thinking. Suddenly, he laughed. "I know who you're talking about! Yeah, wow, that was ages ago. I had gone out looking for dinner, and a woman was just coming out of the saloon as I was walking past. She was so drunk that she tripped and fell right into my arms. Like something from a movie."

"Let me guess," Damien said. "She and Sid were a couple, and he got jealous?"

Theo snorted. "Not a couple, no. She was his sister, apparently. He was right behind her, and he started shouting about how I was taking advantage of a girl who'd had too much to drink. The next thing I knew, he was trying to punch me, even while I was still hanging on to his sister so she wouldn't fall over."

"What happened?" I asked.

"Don't worry." Theo laid a comforting hand on my arm. "I'm a vampire, remember? I got through it without a scratch. I handed the woman off to him, so he suddenly had his arms full and couldn't fight me. While he was trying to get her steady on her feet, I made my exit. He shouted at me the entire time, and I think I offended him because I couldn't stop laughing. The whole thing was so absurd."

"That tracks with what we've heard about Sid's temper," I said. "I guess it's better for Chelsea's boyfriend to be our top suspect than her own son. Thanks, Theo. This is helpful information because it's really giving us a portrait of how Sid behaves."

"If he winds up being the killer, you have to let me put

zombie makeup on you one night," Theo said. "That's my fee for helping you solve a murder."

I opened my mouth to protest, since I was always grossed out by the zombie makeup Theo wore for his role in the lagoon vignette, and I had no desire to look that disgusting, too.

Before I could say anything, though, Theo raised an index finger. "Just think, you won't be able to see yourself, so you can't possibly be horrified by it. However, you'll have the opportunity to know how great it feels to make everyone else feel sick to their stomachs."

I had to concede Theo had a point. I stuck out my hand to shake on it. "Deal."

"You two need to hustle," Damien said, looking at his watch. "You have one minute before tonight's staff meeting."

"Family meeting," I corrected Damien as I headed for the door. Theo didn't even have his boots on yet, so he hollered that he'd catch up.

He caught me five feet before I reached the dining room door, passed me, and led the way inside.

I want vampire speed.

Justine was already making announcements from her usual spot at the podium, and instead of pointing out that Theo and I were tardy, she gave me a look of approval. Sleuthing was, apparently, a worthy excuse for being late. I slid onto an empty bench right as Justine said I'd be posted at the entrance that night.

I made my way to the double front doors once the meeting had concluded. Justine and Clara joined me a couple minutes later, after I had gotten one of the doors propped open and ensured the bucket I dropped ticket stubs into was in its proper place.

"Rose should be here in two minutes," Clara said.

The two minutes came and went, and still, Rose didn't appear. Justine began shifting from one foot to the other. "I have a few things I need to check inside the haunt before we open for the night. Where is she?"

"You go ahead," I told her. "Clara and I will keep watch."

Justine was reluctant to give up, though, and she waited with us another five minutes before she walked out into the circular drive that fronted the Sanctuary. She had to weave her way past the people already lined up at the door, as well as people who were in line at the ticket window.

"No sign of Rose," Justine said when she returned to us. "I thought maybe she was waiting in line, or just running late, but it looks like she's a no-show."

"I'll be here at the front all night, so I'll have someone radio you if she does make it," I assured Justine. "You two go do whatever you need to do."

Clara and Justine both moved off, the disappointment on their faces reflecting my own feelings. Why hadn't Rose shown up?

The Sanctuary was always busy on Friday nights, and I had no shortage of faces to inspect as I tore tickets and welcomed people inside the building. None of those faces, though, belonged to Rose. Clara was the one who relieved me halfway through the night so I could have a short break, and Rose didn't show during her time at the entrance, either.

I was disappointed Rose hadn't shown up, but I was also worried about her. She had seemed scared when we spoke to her at the Grand, and I really hoped she had simply gotten cold feet.

With the front doors locked up after the haunt closed for the night, and the bucket of ticket stubs safely delivered to Zach's office, I was preparing to find Justine and Clara to let them know about our no-show, when Malcolm came flying into the entryway from the direction of the dining room.

My heart seemed to double its pace in an instant. Just as I opened my mouth to ask what was wrong, though, I saw the wild grin on Malcolm's face.

"The egg!" he shouted. "It's hatching!"

CHAPTER TWELVE

Malcolm didn't even stop. He ran right past me, and I heard him shout the same news as he passed Zach's office. Malcolm continued to spread the word while I hurried toward the dining room.

There was already a crowd gathered around the gold birdcage, and I squeezed in between Theo and Gunnar to get a glimpse of what was happening. I could see the phoenix egg, which had grown to about the size of a grapefruit. It seemed to be stretching and flexing.

"Isn't this exciting?" Theo whispered to me.

I turned to answer, then made a gagging noise. Theo had only gotten halfway through removing his zombie makeup, so the top half of his face looked handsome, but his chin and lower cheeks still appeared rotten. Quickly, I returned my gaze to the birdcage. "It is exciting, as long as I don't look at you."

When I felt a firm hand against my lower back, I knew it was Damien. I turned sideways and pulled him in front of me. "That's your dad. Go get yourself a front-row spot."

Wordlessly, Damien slipped through the crowd and sat down on the bench at the table where the birdcage was sitting. Gunnar gave me a nudge forward, and I slid onto the bench next to Damien.

The brilliant red-and-gold egg was flexing again, the top stretching upward. There was a crack that resonated in the silent dining room, and we all leaned forward.

I pulled out my cell phone, thinking I would call Mama to let her know Baxter was hatching, but when I saw the time on the screen, I remembered she would be fast asleep. I was staring at my phone, debating what to do, when Zach called my name softly.

"Don't worry," he said, pointing at the phone raised in his other hand. "I'll send her the video!"

"Thanks!"

During the next few minutes, more cracks appeared in the top of the egg. Suddenly, a pointed yellow shape thrust upward through the shell.

"It's his beak!" Seraphina's tank was positioned close to the birdcage, and she had Baxter's book of phoenix facts in one hand. "He's using it to break up the shell."

Bits of the egg began to break off and fall to the bottom of the birdcage, and soon, I thought I could see something bright red near the beak. In a few moments, a fuzzy little red head emerged, wide yellow eyes blinking out at the world.

Damien gasped, and I wrapped my arms around him. The baby phoenix looked right at Damien and made a low squawking noise. Then, it opened its beak wide, and a tiny ball of flame erupted from it.

"Is that normal?" I asked.

Seraphina waved the book. "It's totally normal for a hatchling to belch fire. As he grows, he'll figure out how to control it."

Maida clapped her hands together, and the sound echoed in the room. She stopped, then clapped again but quietly. Several others followed her lead, wanting to celebrate but not wanting to startle Baxter.

"That's your dad," I told Damien as we continued to

watch the baby phoenix chip away at the egg. Before long, its body began to emerge.

Malcolm's arm slid into my view, and I was surprised to see a champagne flute in his hand. Apparently, he had been prepared for the occasion, and he was handing glasses to everyone. The glasses he gave Mori and Theo, I noticed, had a red liquid in them.

Once we all had a glass in our hands, Malcolm raised his own. He spoke just loudly enough for everyone to hear him. "To our friend and leader, Baxter Shackleford. May this new life cycle be one of joy, love, and adventure!" We all raised our own glasses in response and sipped at our champagne. As I lowered my glass, I looked at Baxter to see him unfold his wings, an orange shimmer on his little red feathers.

Seraphina began issuing orders. "That's the sign that his hatching is complete. Madge, will you please grab that bag of clean ashes over on the other table? Fiona, I need you to scoop out the remnants of the egg. We need to make a clean ash nest for Baxter. Gunnar, grab the fire extinguisher, just in case."

Everyone began to move, either complying with Seraphina's instructions or getting out of the way, except for Damien. He was sitting as still as a statue, gazing at the phoenix.

I squeezed his shoulder. "You okay?" I asked.

"That's my father," Damien answered, his eyes never leaving Baxter. "He was in his phoenix form for such a short time after we rescued him, and I forgot how strange it is to look at a mythical bird and think, *Yeah, that's my dad.*"

"I wonder how long it will be before he can take on his human form again," I mused.

"The book says it can happen once the phoenix reaches full size," Seraphina answered from her tank. "But the book also says something about a power transfer to facilitate it, so I'm not sure what that means."

"I guess we'll find out," Damien said. He finally looked away from Baxter, and a smile broke out on his face. "In the meantime, let's celebrate."

"But quietly!" Seraphina insisted. "We don't want to scare the baby."

I stuck around for another two hours, too excited to go home and sleep. Even Felipe seemed to be in a celebratory mood, because he kept lifting up on his hind legs and running full tilt into anyone who had a free hand for petting him. By the time my watch read three o'clock, I was yawning, and I finally gave in.

Not surprisingly, I overslept on Saturday morning. I had planned to get up early so I could tell Mama the news, but I never heard my alarm clock. I finally woke up at ten, saw the time, and leaped out of bed. I skipped coffee and makeup, and I pulled on the first clothes I could get my hands on. As a result, I found myself rushing up to the motel office dressed in a pair of blue yoga pants and a green silk blouse with a ruffled collar.

When I ran into the office, a man was standing at the check-in counter, so I bounced on my toes impatiently, waiting for him to wrap up his transaction.

I can conjure his hastiness, I realized.

I began to concentrate on how much I wanted the man to leave, focusing on that outcome with all my might. As I stared at the man's back, willing him to finish up, I realized his forest-green suit was well tailored. When he lifted an arm to gesture, I caught the glint of diamonds in his cufflink.

The man at the counter was Leland Porter.

Once I realized that, I stopped conjuring and began eavesdropping.

"There's real value here, for someone willing to invest in some renovations," Leland was saying.

Mama made a *tsk* noise, and he pressed on. "I'm sure you don't have that kind of capital, which is why I'm interested in making you an offer."

I must have unconsciously gasped, because Leland suddenly turned around and looked at me. "Oh, we meet again," he said, eyeing me up and down with a look of distaste. "That's a very…interesting outfit."

"I thought you were staying at the Nightmare Grand," I answered, ignoring the dig on my mismatched clothing.

"I am. I'm not here to check in. I'm here to make an offer to the Daltons."

Behind Leland, Mama was leaning to one side so I could see her clearly, and she gave me an exaggerated wink. She straightened up just as Leland turned around again to face her. "You know, Mr. Porter, Benny and I are getting older, and the day is coming when we won't be able to keep this place up anymore."

"Yes, and you were saying your son won't be taking the motel over from you."

"That's right. Benny and I had planned to keep this place as long as possible before selling. We do love it here. But, I'm willing to hear you out."

I wanted to vault over the countertop and ask Mama what she was thinking. It wasn't that I minded the idea of her and Benny retiring, but I certainly didn't want them selling Cowboy's Corral to a jerk like Leland, who was already talking about renovations. Sure, my shag carpet was old and tacky, but it was a part of the motel's charm. It needed a deep clean, not a replacement.

Mama agreed to sit down for a meeting with Leland sometime in the near future, then shook hands with him. As he walked past me toward the door, I saw the self-satisfied smirk on his face.

The second Leland was gone, I spread my hands. "Mama! You can't really be thinking about selling to that awful man!"

"Of course not!" Mama assured me. "But this gets me on his good side and in his company. Who knows what I might learn about his plans or his possible involvement in Jack's murder?"

The tension flooded out of my body, and I pressed a hand against my forehead as I laughed. "Oh! That's what you meant with the winking."

"You'll have to attend the meeting, too, of course. I'll tell Mr. Porter the motel marketing manager needs to be part of the discussion, as well."

"Good plan. Wow. I haven't had a drop of coffee yet this morning, but I don't think I need it after this."

"That's quite the outfit," Mama commented.

I laughed again. "I threw on the first thing I could find because I wanted to get over here to tell you the good news. Leland drove it right out of my mind. Your brother-in-law has hatched!"

"I know!" Mama grinned and lifted her cell phone. "Zach sent me the video early this morning. Isn't Baxter just the cutest little baby phoenix?"

Mama and I were discussing Baxter's "itty-bitty widdle feathers" when my own phone rang. I was worried as soon as I saw it was Damien. I answered with, "What's wrong?"

"Nothing," Damien said. "Why the worry?"

"Mama and I were just talking about Baxter, so I guess I instantly worried you were calling because something had happened to him."

"My father is fine, and I think he's bigger already. He's definitely louder. But I wasn't calling about him. I was calling to ask if you'd heard about the fire at the general store."

CHAPTER THIRTEEN

"A fire?" I repeated.

"Yeah, sometime late last night," Damien said.

"A fire? Where?" Mama was gripping the Formica countertop and looking at me with wide eyes.

"The general store," I told her.

"Is everyone okay?"

"Is everyone okay?" I relayed to Damien.

"Yes, everyone is… Oh, just put me on speaker phone." I did so, and Damien continued. "No one was hurt. Even the store barely got any damage. It looks like someone broke a front window and set the mannequin displayed there on fire. The fire department arrived before the flames could spread."

"Arson, then," I said.

"It sure looks like it," Damien answered. "Though why anyone would want to set the general store on fire is beyond me."

"Maybe someone got drunk at the saloon and thought it would be funny," Mama speculated, but I could hear the doubt in her voice. It was a far-fetched theory.

"Maybe it has something to do with the general store's landlord, who just got murdered," I suggested.

Mama nodded. "I think that's more likely. Fred Corcoran hasn't tried to hide his dislike for Jack, and maybe someone got the idea that Fred is the killer. This could be someone trying to send a message that they know Fred did it."

I thought about Rose, the hostess at the Nightmare Grand's tearoom, saying she thought Fred had been threatening Jack. If she knew enough to name him as a suspect, then who else might have come to the same conclusion?

I gave Mama a sly grin. "Can you please keep an ear out for town gossip about the fire?"

Mama promised she was on the case, then asked, "Damien, how's Baxter?"

"I was telling Olivia that he seems bigger already. He's —Oh!"

"What?" Mama and I asked in unison.

"Hang on." There was the sound of a few footsteps, then a muffled bang. "Sorry. He just burped fire again, but it was a lot bigger than last night. He caught my kitchen towel on fire."

"Fires everywhere this morning," Mama said. "You have to baby-proof your home, Damien. Don't let Baxter anywhere near your furniture, either."

Damien ended the call, saying he was going to clear a wide space in the middle of his living room floor so Baxter's belches couldn't set anything else ablaze. At least the home itself couldn't burn down, since Damien lived in a former copper mine. The bare rock surfaces could take the heat.

Maybe that's why Baxter bought Sonny's Folly Mine in the first place.

Once I was off the phone with Damien, Mama told me she wasn't the only one with a meeting to look forward to. "Lucy has her weekly tutoring session with Vivian this afternoon. I thought you might want to be a fly on the wall for it."

"I'll definitely go check in with those two. But first, I should probably do something about my fashion choices."

"And brush your hair. I didn't want to say anything, but it's a bit of a mess, honey."

"Coffee first, then hair."

I was tempted to go check out the aftermath of the general store fire for myself, but I was also looking forward to a few quiet hours at home. It was nice to crack open the window and leisurely sip my coffee.

By the time I began my walk to the Sanctuary to check in on Lucy's session with Vivian, I was looking much more put-together. I had swapped my yoga pants for a pair of jeans and that same green silk blouse, and a lightweight black cardigan completed my outfit.

It took about twenty minutes to walk to the Sanctuary, and halfway there, I peeled off my cardigan. The weather wasn't anywhere near as hot as it would be during the summer, but things were definitely warming up. Still, it was a nice day for walking, and I arrived at the Sanctuary feeling energized.

The front doors of the old building were usually locked during the day, so I knocked as loudly as I dared, not wanting to wake up all the people I knew were upstairs, asleep in their apartments. Malcolm was the one who answered the door, and he stifled a yawn as he wished me a good afternoon.

"Just getting up?" I asked as he stepped back to let me in.

"We polished off the last of the champagne at five o'clock this morning, then we sat around and chatted until the vampires had to go to bed."

"Party animals."

"I assume you're here to see how Lucy is progressing. Come on. I'd like to see for myself."

Malcolm led me to a small room that was down the

same hallway as Zach's and Damien's offices. Like Damien's office, the room we entered was an interior one with no windows. It was lit only by half a dozen candles burning on a round table in the center of the room, and I had to pause to let my eyes adjust.

As I shut the door behind me, I heard Lucy let out a frustrated huff. She and Vivian were sitting across from each other at the table, and although Lucy's back was to me, I could see the tension in her posture.

"I can't do it!" Lucy whined.

"Tough session?" I asked gently.

Vivian glanced up at me, her face looking ethereal in the glow of the candlelight. "We're trying to call Lucille, but if she's hearing Lucy, she's not responding."

I gazed around the room. Since my eyes had gotten used to the low light, I could see the old photographs hanging on the walls. Most of them showed hospital staff, with nurses in long white dresses and doctors with bushy beards and wire-rim glasses.

"I thought you held séances in the basement," I commented. We had once attended a séance with Vivian that had been down there.

"Only if there are a lot of us. I use this office when it's just one or two others, because it's so cozy." Vivian sat back in her chair and stretched her arms over her head, then adjusted the navy-blue bandana tied around her hair. "Lucy, do you want to try again?"

"I'm not sure there's any point. I'm not good enough to do this."

It was rare for Lucy to be down about anything, and I was concerned to hear the defeat in her voice. She was anxious to talk to the ghost of her great-aunt Lucille, and she had been working hard to communicate with the Vanishing Girls at school. I could see how it would be a

94

frustrating situation for a ten-year-old who was still in the early stages of learning how to be a psychic medium.

To my surprise, it was Malcolm who stepped in to offer advice. He knelt down next to Lucy's chair. "It takes a lot of patience to train our minds," he said, his voice full of sympathy. "I once had to be very patient, too, when I was training my mind to grow. It's hard, but you have to keep trying, and little by little, you'll begin to see the results. It's worth the effort, in the long run."

Vivian and I looked at each other. We both knew Malcolm was talking about his work to overcome his predatory nature. As a wendigo, Malcolm's instinct was to hunt down humans. Baxter had helped him learn to overcome his monstrous side. And, I was certain, that had been a lot more difficult than learning to communicate with ghosts.

"Will you help me?" Lucy asked. She still sounded doubtful.

"Of course." Malcolm put his hand palm-up on the table, and Lucy placed hers on top. Her hand nearly disappeared as Malcolm's fingers closed around it. Malcolm extended his other hand. "Olivia?"

I stepped up next to Malcolm and took his hand, and Lucy closed her eyes in concentration. A few silent minutes crept by, then Lucy sighed. "It felt better that time. Sort of like a buzzing feeling in my brain."

"Why don't we ask Damien to join us?" I suggested. I dropped Malcolm's hand and pulled my phone out to text him. "I bet your cousin would like to lend his assistance, too."

Mama had a theory that the combined supernatural powers of Damien, Lucy, and me helped Lucille make her presence known, and I hoped having Damien with us would be the last nudge Lucy needed to make contact. I waited for a text back from him while Vivian gave Lucy a few pointers.

Instead of a text, I got Damien himself. The door opened, and he walked in with Baxter's cage dangling from one hand. Once Lucy's squeal of delight at the sight of the phoenix died down, he said, "Perfect timing. I just got here to take care of a few things."

"How was your drive?" I asked with a lopsided smile. The birdcage didn't fit into Damien's Corvette, so he had been taking Baxter back and forth between the mine and the Sanctuary in Theo's compact SUV. Damien would tell anyone who would listen how much of a burden it was not to be behind the wheel of his sports car for that short drive. Naturally, we were all teasing him mercilessly about it.

"You can comfort me later," Damien answered, his own smile matching mine. "First, let's see what we can do for Lucy."

Soon, all five of us were gathered at the table, our hands linked. Lucy closed her eyes again and began to breathe deeply.

Vivian suddenly made a small happy noise, and she beamed at Lucy, who still had her eyes shut tight. *She's here*, Vivian mouthed to the rest of us.

"Miss Olivia," Lucy said after a few moments, "Great-aunt Lucille says her necklace looks good on you."

Damien had given me the necklace shortly after I had arrived in Nightmare. The silver chain had two small charms on it, a cross and a pentagram, and Damien had explained there were powerful protection spells on them. Baxter had given the necklace to Lucille many decades before, and Damien had passed it on to me, believing I had a knack for getting myself into trouble and needed all the protection I could get.

He wasn't wrong.

"And she says she'd be happy to go to the energy pool,"

Lucy continued. "I just asked her in my mind if she'd like to swim in it."

"Suggest to her that we go tonight, shortly after dark," Damien said.

Lucy was silent for another minute, then she nodded. "She says okay." She opened her eyes. "I think she went away again."

Vivian nodded. "Her presence isn't here anymore. Lucy, you did great! I'm so proud of you."

"We can take Tanner and McCrory with us, too," Damien said. "They'll enjoy going to the spring again."

"But if we go at dark, we'll miss the opening of the haunt," I pointed out.

"It will be fine if we miss the first hour or so. By going early, Lucy can come with us."

Lucy's face brightened, but Damien quickly added, "If your parents say it's okay."

Not only was Nick open to the idea when he came to pick up Lucy, but he asked to go, too. He wanted the chance to hang out with Tanner and McCrory, saying it was still surreal to talk to a couple of ghosts—and Wild West legends, at that.

We were still at the Sanctuary's entrance after handing Lucy over to her dad when Justine and Clara joined us. Justine jangled her car keys, and Clara grabbed my hand. "Let's go!"

"Go where?" I asked.

Clara still had a tight grip on my hand, and I began to follow her out the door as I nodded goodbye to Damien, Malcolm, and Vivian. "My aunt just called and said there's drama at the coffee shop, and it might have to do with the murder!"

CHAPTER FOURTEEN

"What kind of drama?" I asked as Clara and Justine led me in the direction of Justine's car.

"My aunt didn't say. She just said we need to get there quick." Clara sounded excited, and I knew she was enjoying getting to have a hand in looking into Jack Wiley's murder. Apparently, so was her aunt.

It was a good thing I had my seatbelt on, because Justine drove like she was in a race. When she pulled out of the dirt parking lot of the Sanctuary and onto the narrow lane that led to the street, the rear tires of the car slewed sideways, and only the seatbelt kept me from sliding across the back seat. Clara let out a scream, and Justine laughed nervously as she got the car heading in the right direction.

"Sorry, you two. I'll slow down."

Except, she didn't. We hit a bump so hard I instinctively grabbed the back of the passenger seat, bracing myself for an impact.

When Justine stopped at the crossroads, Clara reached over and put a hand on the steering wheel. "We'll never find out what's going on if we're dead," she said.

"I'm not driving that badly," Justine said defensively. Still, she eased onto the road, and if she didn't drive the speed limit all the way to High Noon Boulevard, she was at least close to it.

We found a parking spot one street over from the tourist street, which wasn't an easy feat on a Saturday. Luckily, a car had just been pulling out of a spot as we arrived, and Justine dove into it before anyone else could. She and Clara jumped out of the car while I scrambled at a slower pace, but soon, all three of us were speed-walking toward The Caffeinated Cadaver.

Walking inside the coffee shop usually felt nice, like being welcomed into a cozy spot full of delicious smells and comfortable places to lounge. On this occasion, it felt daunting. People sitting in the chairs were reading or chatting in small groups, but there was a palpable tension.

My eyes landed on a tall man with a broad chest and a face that was probably nice-looking when there wasn't a scowl plastered on it. He was standing near the counter, and the barista behind it was pressed back against the wall, trying to put as much room between herself and the man as possible.

The angry man was Sid, Chelsea Gentry's boyfriend.

Another man was walking toward us, and I realized with a start it was Fred Corcoran. The manager of the general store had a similar scowl on his face, and as he passed by me, I heard him mutter, "I just wanted a coffee. I wasn't looking for a fight."

Justine, Clara, and I had all stepped to the side to let Fred pass, and after he had disappeared out the door, I returned my attention to Sid. Clearly, he and Fred had been the source of the drama, but I had no idea what the two of them had been fighting about.

"We missed all the fun," Justine said under her breath.

"Who's the big guy?" Clara asked.

I began to answer, but, even as I did so, I spotted Chelsea walking toward Sid. His face softened ever so slightly, and Chelsea put her hand into his.

"Oh, so that's her boyfriend," Clara said, answering her own question.

"He's gigantic," Justine commented. "Someone of that size would have had no problem bashing Jack over the head."

"But why would he kill the guy in his own girlfriend's bakery?" Clara asked. "That would automatically make her a suspect."

"Maybe Sid didn't plan to kill Jack, but his notorious temper got the best of him when he saw Jack there in the bakery," I speculated. "Or, perhaps, he's not the killer. Only one way to find out."

Since we had missed whatever confrontation had occurred between Sid and Fred, I wasn't even going to bring it up. Instead, I walked up to Chelsea as if nothing had just happened and said, "Oh, Chelsea, I'm glad to see you. I was going to check in and see how you were doing."

Chelsea glanced at me, then at Sid. "Olivia, it's good to see you. Sid, you remember Olivia, Mama's friend."

Sid just stared at me, but at least he was no longer scowling.

"Anyway," Chelsea continued, "I'd be better if we knew who killed Jack. Can you believe Fred Corcoran just accused Sid of doing it? And in front of everyone here! The whole town will be saying Sid did it by sundown." Chelsea's breath hitched, and I worried she might start crying.

"How did Fred come to that conclusion?" I asked.

"It's no secret I didn't like Jack." Sid's tone was bitter, and his lips pressed together into a thin line. "Jack didn't treat Chelsea well when they were married, and he didn't treat her well as her landlord. Some people were scared of him, but I wasn't. I stood up to him."

"But Sid didn't kill him!" Chelsea interjected.

"Plus," Sid continued, "there was that whole incident last Christmas. I told him Quinn was just—"

"Jack had run-ins with a lot of people in Nightmare." Chelsea nodded at me. "I appreciate you looking into the murder for me, Olivia. I don't want people in this town thinking me or Sid are guilty."

"I'm sorry you had to deal with Fred's outburst," I said politely.

Chelsea and Sid moved off, and it was only then I spotted Quinn. He had been standing a short distance behind his mother, looking just as disgruntled as Sid. I wondered if he, too, was angry at Fred for making such a public accusation, or if his ire was directed at Sid. I knew Quinn and Jack hadn't had a good relationship, but how was Quinn dealing with his mother's new boyfriend?

"While we're here," Clara said as we watched the trio head out, "we may as well get coffee."

Clara and I had very different ideas of what it meant to have coffee. I liked a latte, but Clara's order involved flavored syrup, whipped cream, and even sprinkles. The stuff in her cup looked more like a melted ice cream sundae than coffee.

Justine and I both shook our heads and laughed as we sat down in one corner of the coffee shop. "Fairies," Justine muttered.

Clara drank almost half of her beverage in one gulp. She wiped a dollop of whipped cream off her upper lip, then said, "We should stroll by the general store once we're done here."

Justine and I were quick to agree to that plan, but she and I were determined to drink our coffees in a more leisurely fashion. Eventually, though, we headed down the boardwalk until we were standing in front of the remains of the general store's charred display window. A sheet of thick plastic had been nailed in place over the broken glass, but it was easy to spot the burned wooden boards along the top edge.

"Can you believe someone would do this to my store?" Fred Corcoran stepped up next to me. He was still scowling, and his hands were curled into fists.

I almost asked Fred if he was speaking to me, because we didn't know each other, and he wasn't even looking in my direction. His gaze was on the fire damage. Gently, I said, "It's a shame. I hope it's easy to fix."

"Oh, I'm not worried about that." Fred's hands relaxed, and he hooked his thumbs into his brown leather belt. "I'm more interested in seeing the guilty party arrested."

"Do you have any idea who might have done this?"

"Someone who wants me to stay quiet," Fred answered without hesitation. "Someone who knows that I hear about everything that happens in this town, and they don't want me saying anything that might make them look like Jack's killer."

Before I could respond, Fred stalked into his store, brushing past a couple of startled-looking tourists who were on their way out with full shopping bags.

"I wonder if Fred is right," I said once he had disappeared.

"Whether or not the fire was set as a warning, the damage really isn't that bad," Justine noted. "An old wooden structure like this could have easily gone up in minutes, so it's lucky the fire was extinguished so quickly."

"Damien said it was a mannequin in the display that was torched," I said. "If it had been the building itself, I imagine the outcome would have been very different."

The three of us stood in silence for a moment, and I was imagining what could have been while feeling grateful the damage was so minimal. The store was right in the middle of High Noon Boulevard, and it was one of the precious buildings from Nightmare's days as a mining boomtown.

In fact, I was willing to bet McCrory had shopped there back in his days as sheriff, though he probably hadn't been buying overpriced T-shirts and keychains.

I was making a mental note to ask McCrory about his history with the building—and whether or not Tanner had ever tried to rob the place—when a man who slightly resembled McCrory walked up to us. He was wearing all black, including his cowboy hat and duster.

"Justine Abbott! It's been ages!" He was beaming at Justine.

"Riley! Hey!" Justine hugged the man, then turned to Clara and me. "Riley and I went to high school together."

Another man stepped up next to Riley. He was also wearing a cowboy hat and duster, and his look reminded me of Tanner, except this man didn't have a red bandana over his mouth and nose.

"Oh! Tanner and McCrory!" It had finally clicked for me. "You two do the re-enactments of their shootout."

"That's right." Riley smiled proudly. "The last show of the day is in half an hour, if you ladies would like to stick around for it."

"We've got to get back to work," Justine said, "but I've seen you two pretend to kill each other plenty of times."

The man playing Tanner nodded toward the ruined window. "It's a shame about the fire. I hope they get it repaired soon, because the tourists don't want to see a mess like that. It ruins the illusion."

"The illusion that we've all time-traveled to the eighteen eighties?" Clara asked.

"Exactly."

Riley narrowed his eyes as he looked at the store. "That display window has been nothing but trouble since it went in last year."

"Why?" I couldn't imagine what kind of scandal a pane of glass could create.

"We spend a lot of time out here, taking photos with tourists and chatting with people. I've heard three different people yell at Fred, the manager, about that stupid window. One of the people who made a fuss about it was that murdered landlord."

CHAPTER FIFTEEN

"Jack Wiley owns this building," I pointed out. "Or, he did own it, before he was killed. Why would he yell about a change he'd made to his own property?"

"Because he didn't make the change," Riley said. "Fred brought out a contractor early on a Sunday morning, and by the time the landlord found out what was happening, it was too late."

"Fred was dumb enough to make an alteration to the building without asking Jack first?" Justine shook her head. "No wonder the two of them didn't get along."

"It wasn't just Jack who was angry about the window," the man playing Tanner said. "The guy who runs the Nightmare Grand is part of the Nightmare Historic Society, and he pitched a fit because the window's design didn't match the historic guidelines for High Noon Boulevard."

"Plus," Riley said, "some big dude stomped over here and started yelling at Fred about how the window had made Jack mad, and he was taking it out on all of his tenants. The two of them had a shouting match in front of dozens of people."

"Big dude?" Justine stretched a hand up, like she was measuring someone's height. "Looks like he could knock you out in one punch?"

Both men nodded.

"That would be Sid," Clara said.

It suddenly made a lot more sense why Fred had marched into The Caffeinated Cadaver and accused Sid of murdering Jack. The two of them apparently had a habit of public accusations. And, I figured, Fred also suspected Sid had set the fire.

What didn't make sense was the news that Ellis, the manager of the Nightmare Grand, had been mad at Fred about the window. If that were the case, then it didn't seem likely the two men had teamed up to threaten Jack, as the hostess at the tearoom had implied. It would have made more sense if Ellis and Jack had been working together to subdue Fred.

Justine must have been working out the same connections in her mind, because she abruptly said, "We have to make a stop before we get back to the Sanctuary."

"Oh, do all three of you work there?" The man playing Tanner was looking right at Clara. "I'm Preston, by the way. I've been meaning to make it out to your haunt. It's been years since I last went."

Clara gave him a shy smile. "We'd love to see you there."

I suddenly had an image of Clara dating the spitting image of Butch Tanner, and I wondered what the real Tanner would think of it.

"Gentlemen, you've been very helpful," I said. "Thank you. And, for the record, your performance was one of the first things I saw when I arrived in Nightmare. It made quite an impression, and I plan to catch one of your shows again soon."

In fact, I wanted to bring Tanner and McCrory to see it, so they could tell me whether or not the re-creation was historically accurate. I just had to figure out a way to get the ghosts to High Noon Boulevard without any tourists spotting them.

We said goodbye to Riley and Preston, and as soon as they had moved off, I said lightly, "So, tearoom?"

Justine nodded. "I want to talk to Rose, because her theory about Ellis and Fred makes no sense."

"He was cute," Clara said in a breathy voice.

"He's human," Justine noted.

"Don't burst my bubble." Clara looked mostly human, but her violet eyes and pointed ears were a giveaway that she was a fairy. She usually wore her silvery hair down to cover her ears, but if she started dating a human, it would only be a matter of time before he noticed she was a bit different.

Justine seemed to realize her error, because she slung an arm around Clara's shoulders. "I'm dating a human, too."

"But you are a human."

"Yes, but I'm a telekinetic human. Luis is just a normal human. Now that he knows about the supernatural world, we're making it work. If you and Preston wind up having the great love story of the century, I'm sure you two will find a way to make it work, too."

Clara giggled. "I'm not looking to marry the guy! I just thought it could be fun to go out with a cute cowboy."

I elbowed Clara playfully. "If you're looking for a cute cowboy who's not going to be blindsided by the supernatural, Tanner is single."

"No ghosts," Clara said firmly. "I prefer my men living."

We spent the short walk to the Nightmare Grand discussing the pros and cons of dating a ghost. Soon, though, we were walking into the tearoom once again.

Rose was there, at her spot behind the stand at the front of the room. She flashed a wide smile at us, but it disappeared as soon as she realized who she was greeting. Her voice shook as she asked, "Table for three?"

"We were hoping to talk to you," I said gently. "We were worried when you didn't show up last night."

Rose averted her eyes. "Sorry about that. Something came up."

"We're glad you're okay," Justine said.

Rose continued to stare at a spot on the wallpaper. "Table for three?"

"No. We were nearby, so we just wanted to check on you." Clara sounded as disappointed as I felt, because there was no way Rose was going to get into a discussion with us about the mysterious Ellis, Fred, and Jack triangle. "Like Justine said, we're happy to see you're okay."

I tried to give Rose my best reassuring look, but she was still staring at the wall as we left.

She's terrified.

We were trooping past the door to the Grand's offices when Ellis came hurrying out of it. "Oh, ladies, hello again!" he said. "Were you coming to visit me?"

"We were just down the street, so I wanted to stop inside to see this place again," I said. It was the first viable excuse for our presence that popped into my head. "I just can't get over how gorgeous it is."

Ellis looked around the lobby with a proud expression. "We put a lot of hard work into keeping this old gal looking her best."

"We just saw the aftermath of the fire at the general store," Justine said. "I can't understand why anyone would want to do something like that to one of these old places."

Ellis shook his head sadly. "That beautiful historic building. It could have been so much worse. I'm grateful it was only that awful window display that burned. I spent two hours this morning drafting a letter on behalf of the Nightmare Historic Society, expressing our condolences and advising how it can be restored to its original look without being overly costly."

I gave what I hoped came off as a teasing smile. "Ellis, did you set that fire to get rid of the modern window?"

Ellis barked out a laugh. "You think I would risk damaging one of Nightmare's legacy buildings? I've dedicated my life to preserving these places and the stories they have to tell. I love this town and its history."

"So do we," Clara said. "In fact, we're going to catch the next shootout re-enactment."

"Oh, are we?" Justine snickered.

"Ellis, it was nice to bump into you," I said. "We'll see you later."

"They're both single," Ellis called after us. When we all turned to him with surprised looks, he grinned sheepishly. "I work with Riley and Preston a lot for historic events, and I figure there's only one reason local ladies would be so eager to catch their show."

Clara's face turned a shade of red I hadn't even known was possible to achieve, but her grin was as big as Ellis's. "Thanks for the intel."

Justine and I agreed to Clara's plan, despite Justine's reluctance. The only thing that got Justine to agree was Clara's promise to help her speed through her to-do list as soon as they got back to the Sanctuary.

We made our way back to High Noon Boulevard, where tourists were already crowding on both sides of the street to see the final shootout of the day. I knew from my first visit to that street, though, that the action didn't begin on the street itself. Instead, it began with a shouting match on the boardwalk.

Before long, Riley and Preston were exchanging barbs. Preston had completed his transformation into Butch Tanner, adding the bandana and looking remarkably like the person he was portraying. He had the same glittering, mischievous eyes as Tanner.

The two men continued shouting, until McCrory

suggested there was only one way for them to settle their dispute. They both stalked into the center of the street, their boots kicking up dust as they counted off ten paces each. Then, they stood facing each other, each man with a hand hovering near his gun holster.

The crowd was absolutely silent as the seconds stretched. Riley and Preston had locked eyes with each other, their bodies perfectly still. Preston's fingers twitched, and suddenly, he and Riley had their six-shooters out and aimed at each other. There were three loud bangs as the blanks in the guns went off, and both actors staggered before hitting the ground.

A roar of cheers and applause erupted from the crowd, and I joined in with enthusiasm. The fact that I knew the real Tanner and McCrory made watching the show a special treat, and now that I had met the actors portraying them, I had another personal connection to it.

The crowd began to break up, and a line formed of people wanting to snap a photo with Riley and Preston. As I watched, a laugh erupted from my mouth. "I love this town," I enthused.

"I remember when you thought it was pretty weird and couldn't wait to leave," Justine teased.

"I still think Nightmare is weird, and I wouldn't have it any other way."

"This town isn't weird. It's wonderful," a male voice said. I turned to see Emmett Kline standing at my elbow. "Hi, ladies. Olivia, I'm glad I saw you here. I've got some information, but I'm not sure if it's worth passing on to the police. Maybe you can tell me if it's relevant to Jack's murder or not."

I gestured toward Emmett. "Let's hear it."

"Remember when I mentioned that historic building I'd thought you and Damien might be interested in? Well, I just found out Beef Bilsby was in a bidding war for it with

Jack Wiley and that rich out-of-towner. I guess it's a good thing you and Damien didn't want it, after all, because Beef won the war."

I nodded. "I remember you mentioning the building, but I don't know who Beef is. Do we have yet another suspect in Jack's murder?"

"Oh, I thought you knew! Beef is what some of us old-timers in this town call Chelsea's boyfriend, Sid."

CHAPTER SIXTEEN

"Sid and Jack were in a bidding war for real estate," I mused. I absently chewed my bottom lip while I let that information sink in. "That means their enmity wasn't just about Chelsea."

"Rumor has it that Beef—Sid, as you know him—paid far more than he wanted for the place," Emmett said. "Even once Jack was dead and out of the running, he still had that rich guy to deal with."

"Leland Porter." I recalled Leland telling Damien he was looking at a two-story place he would use as a winter home upstairs and a retail space or similar downstairs. That had probably been the very piece of real estate Emmett had mentioned to us. "I didn't know Sid was into real estate, as well."

Emmett waved a hand dismissively. "As I understand it, this was his first experience with it. Maybe he was in it just to ruin Jack's plans for the place, or maybe he figured if Jack could make a living as a landlord, then so could he."

I began ticking off things against Sid. "He's dating Chelsea, who was mistreated by Jack, both as a spouse and a landlord. Plus, Sid is known to have a temper. And, most recently, he'd been in a real estate bidding war with Jack. No wonder Fred accused him of being the killer."

Emmett's eyes widened. "Fred, over at the general store?"

"Right in front of everyone sitting inside The Caffeinated Cadaver, apparently," Justine said. She had been silently listening to the conversation, but Clara had wandered off.

"Interesting. Thank you. You've convinced me this information is definitely worth passing along to the police. I'll head there now."

"I'll go with you," Justine offered. "I can say hi to Luis."

"I, on the other hand, am heading home," I said. "Justine, keep an eye on Clara, or she's going to be slurping down sugary drinks with an outlaw in no time."

Emmett stopped me before I could go. He leaned in close and said in a voice only loud enough for Justine and me, "Does that gargoyle ever do freelance work? I could use someone to get aerial shots of properties."

Justine and I both laughed. "Only if you want night shots," she said. "He can't risk flying during the day, because he might be seen."

As I began to walk away, I heard Emmett ask Justine, "What about the fairy? Does she have wings hidden somewhere?"

I used the time during my walk back to Cowboy's Corral to think about everything we had learned and experienced in what I had thought would be a short outing to the coffee shop. I was feeling so drained I possibly needed more coffee, but I would do it in the peace and quiet of my apartment.

Damien called me after I'd gotten home to check in and to let me know we'd be meeting Nick and Lucy in his office at six thirty that evening. I had been so wrapped up in following leads for Jack's murder that I had totally forgotten we were going to take Lucille to the energy spring that night. I told Damien I'd be there, then went back to my quiet coffee and contemplation.

I got to the Sanctuary that night shortly before the family meeting, which meant I would have some time with Damien before the night's adventure really got started. The birdcage was the first thing I noticed when I walked into Damien's office.

"He's bigger," I said. It felt like an understatement. Baxter still didn't look like a fully grown bird, but he was well beyond the hatchling phase already. As if he knew I was talking about him, he turned his eyes toward me and belched a fireball the size of an orange.

"And louder." Damien got up and moved around his desk so he could give me a kiss. He was dressed more casually than usual, and I figured his jeans and black T-shirt were so he didn't have to worry about snagging an expensive suit on any plants out by the energy spring.

Damien typically stayed in his office during each evening's pre-work meeting, so I was surprised when he said he would come with me to the dining room. "I need to hand my father off to someone," he explained. "Plus, I've asked Justine to announce what we're doing tonight so they know why a few of us are missing."

I was ready, then, when Justine told the staff that some of us were attempting to give Lucille's ghost an energy boost that night. What I hadn't been prepared for was the way every head in the dining room turned to look at Damien and me. I caught a lot of hopeful expressions, even from the many people who had arrived at the Sanctuary long after Lucille had ceased to exist.

We were bombarded with well-wishers once the meeting wrapped up. Mori went one step further. "Take him with you," she said, gesturing toward Felipe. He was lying on his back, his front paws firmly clamped around the hem of Morgan's long black dress.

"If you tear the lace, I'll work a spell to turn you into a vegetarian!" Morgan's tone was threatening, but her wrinkled face had a smile on it.

"You'll be out wandering in the middle of nowhere," Mori continued. "Felipe can be extra security for you."

"Are you being generous, or just trying to pass your misbehaving chupacabra off on us for a while?" I teased.

Mori's lips curved upward. "Both."

Damien and I were walking out of the dining room when we spotted Nick and Lucy heading down the hall toward us. Lucy began to skip, stopping only when she was inches away. "Where's the mermaid?" she asked.

"Probably in the lagoon vignette already," I told her. "Some people are still getting into costume, but most are already settling into their spots inside the haunt."

Lucy pointed in the direction of the haunt's entrance. "Let's go to the lagoon, then."

"Lucy," Nick said, "we're here to help your great-aunt, remember?"

"I know," Lucy said, her shoulders drooping.

"I have to go get the six-shooter box," Damien said. "Why don't all of you go say hello to Seraphina while I grab it and get Felipe on his leash? I'll meet you in the entryway in five minutes."

Lucy bounced on the balls of her feet. "Yay!" She turned and began to head for the haunt's entrance.

"I'd say I could lead the way," I told Nick as we followed at a slower pace, "but she might know her way around here even better than I do."

As expected, Seraphina was already inside the water tank in the lagoon vignette, and she was delighted to see Lucy again. Lucy still believed Seraphina was a human woman dressed as a mermaid, and I wondered how she would react someday when she learned her favorite Nightmare Sanctuary employee was an actual siren.

Damien was already waiting for us when we emerged from the haunt into the entryway. He had the wooden six-shooter box tucked under one arm, and Felipe was straining against his purple leash, which Damien was holding tightly in his hand.

Vivian was just coming down the staircase, chatting with Tanner and McCrory. Lucy bounded up to her excitedly while the ghosts both lifted their hats in greeting.

Damien decided to drive Theo's SUV, so we could all cram into one vehicle. Damien and Nick sat up front, while Vivian and I easily fit next to Lucy in the back seat. Felipe had plenty of room behind us, and the ghosts were left to sit wherever they pleased. After some debate, they agreed to settle in the back with Felipe.

Tanner leaned forward until his face was between Lucy's and mine. "Turn right at the gallows," he called to Damien.

"No, go straight at the gallows," McCrory said.

Damien raised a hand and glanced at the ghosts in the rearview mirror. "Not this again." He pointed at his cell phone, which was propped up on the center console. "I marked the spot when we were there before, so I have the directions right here."

Tanner swooped through the back seat, between Lucy and me, sending a wave of cold through my side. "Look at that tiny map! Wow. You know, it was a lot harder to find your way around back when I was living. We didn't have all this fancy modern stuff."

"Mister Damien, can you please turn on the heat?" Lucy called.

"Tanner, you're making us cold," I scolded.

"Oops. Sorry, ladies." Tanner returned to his spot in the back while Lucy briskly rubbed her arms.

When we arrived, Vivian sucked in a breath, even

before Damien had turned off the car. "Oh, I can feel it already. This is going to be exciting."

Lucy said she didn't feel anything, but as we made the walk to the energy spring, she suddenly began to giggle. "It feels like the hair on my arms is standing up," she explained. "It's like when it's cold out, and you walk across the carpet in your socks."

Vivian laughed. "That's the perfect analogy. You're feeling the energy radiating from this spot. Let's hope Lucille can sense it, too."

Tanner and McCrory were just as excited to return to the spring as they had been on their previous visit, but Vivian asked them to hold in their yells of delight for a bit so she and Lucy could try to contact Lucille. Not only did the ghosts quiet down, but they both stood still. McCrory even removed his hat, as if we were at some formal event.

"Go ahead, Lucy," Vivian said.

Lucy drew in a deep breath, then blew it out in a rush. "Great-aunt Lucille, are you here? Do you want to come play in this energy pool?"

Felipe let out a sharp yelp, and I looked down to see him staring at a spot behind Lucy.

Damien, I realized, was turned in the same direction. His mouth was slightly open, and Felipe's leash slipped from his fingers.

I turned to follow Damien's gaze and saw a woman standing behind Lucy. She was barely visible, and a slight shimmer kept my eyes from focusing on her. It didn't matter, though. I recognized her, anyway, from the old photograph I had seen at the mine Damien lived in.

Beside me, I felt Damien shift. "Mom!"

CHAPTER SEVENTEEN

Lucille beamed at Damien. Her mouth formed the words, *My son,* but there was no sound.

"We found Dad," Damien told her. "And you helped us do it. He's safe now. Thank you."

Lucille nodded.

"Can you talk?" I asked.

In answer, Lucille drifted forward until she was standing next to Lucy. She looked down at her great-niece silently.

"She says she's not strong enough yet," Lucy told us. She tapped her fingers against her temple. "She can talk in my mind, but not in real life."

There was a loud sound of footsteps pounding against the packed dirt behind me, and I whirled around. *Maybe we'll need Felipe, after all,* I thought as I waited for whomever was running toward us to emerge from the darkness.

To my enormous relief and surprise, it was Gunnar who appeared, but he wasn't alone. He was carrying Mama in his arms.

Mama pointed toward us. "I can't believe you all were going to leave me out of the fun! Nick told me the plan earlier, and I thought I could wait for your report, but I decided I couldn't wait to find out what happened. I had to come see for myself."

Gunnar gingerly put Mama down. "She showed up at the Sanctuary and demanded directions to this place, plus an escort. She wasn't sure-footed out here in the dark, so I carried her from her car."

"I didn't want to come alone," Mama said. "I knew Gunnar would see me safely here, though I told him there was no way I was going to fly with him."

Gunnar got a panicked expression on his face at that comment, but he relaxed when he looked at Nick and Lucy, who were both focused on the ghost of Lucille. There would be no need to tell them gargoyles were real, and Gunnar wasn't simply wearing an incredibly realistic costume.

Mama was looking around, and she suddenly gasped. "Oh, there she is!" She walked toward Lucille while Damien explained that Lucille wouldn't be able to talk.

"That doesn't matter," Mama said, her voice shaking as she stepped up beside her son and granddaughter. "Oh, my sweet sister. It's so good to see you."

Lucille blew a kiss at Mama, then clasped her hands together under her chin. If she had been human, I expected we would have seen tears streaming down her face.

Mama patted her voluminous hair. "I went a little gray. Put on a few pounds, too."

Lucille looked at Lucy, who relayed, "She says you look beautiful, Grandma!"

"I'm sorry we didn't tell you our plan, Mama," I said. "We didn't know if it would work or not, and we didn't want you to get your hopes up."

"I imagine this is beyond anyone's expectations." Mama reached back, her palm upturned. "Damien, come here." She took his hand as he stepped forward. He hadn't said a word since greeting his mom, and he was still staring at her with a look of shock.

"Isn't he handsome?" Mama enthused. "And such a good man, Lucille. You must be so proud of him."

Lucille lifted a hand toward Damien's cheek, even though her fingers couldn't make physical contact with him.

"Dad's going to be so happy to see you," Damien said, "though, as I'm sure you know, he's in his bird form right now."

Lucy shook her head. "She says she's not strong enough to go back with you yet. She needs to stay here for a while."

"The energy here will help revitalize her," Vivian agreed. "The longer she's here, the stronger she'll get."

"But I need your help with the Vanishing Girls." Lucy gave Lucille a pleading look. After a few moments of silence, Lucy simply said, "Okay. I'll try."

"Try what, honey?" Mama asked.

"Lucille says I don't need her help. I should just talk to the ghosts and be their friend, and they'll tell me what they need."

Lucille's form began to fade.

"It's going to take a while before Lucille has absorbed enough of this energy to stay visible," Vivian explained. "We should let her rest and recharge."

Lucille waved just before she disappeared, and Lucy called after her, "See you soon!"

Mama wrapped her arms around Damien's body, and the two of them hugged for a long time. Eventually, they stepped apart, and Damien reluctantly said it was time to go. Lucy grabbed Felipe's leash and tugged gently. He was still staring expectantly at the spot Lucille had vacated.

As we made our way back to the car, Damien asked Gunnar, "Aren't you supposed to be working?"

Gunnar gestured toward Mama, who was walking ahead of us with Nick. "There's no arguing with that lady!

But I'm leaving her in good hands, so I'll head back to the haunt." He hurried ahead of us and soon disappeared into the darkness, so Nick and Lucy wouldn't see him launch into the air.

Mama had driven herself to the energy spring, and when Damien expressed his surprise that she had managed to find the place, she said Malcolm had given her directions based on what McCrory had told him.

Nick offered to ride with Mama as she followed us back toward town, and she took the six-shooter box with her so Tanner and McCrory could keep them company.

We got twenty feet down the road when something massive appeared in the headlights. Vivian let out a shriek, and I instinctively braced for a collision. Damien slammed on the brakes and came to a stop just a foot away from Gunnar, who had landed on the road right in front of us.

Good thing Nick is riding with Mama. Hopefully, neither he nor Lucy had noticed Gunnar came from above us rather than the side of the road.

Behind us, I could hear the squeal of Mama's tires as she tried to avoid plowing into the back of our car.

Damien opened the driver's-side door in time for me to hear Gunnar shout, "Fire! At the bakery!"

"How bad?" Damien called.

"I'm not sure. I saw the flames and the fire truck already on its way, but you'd better go check it out in case this has to do with the murder."

"On our way," Damien said. He slammed the door shut and hit the gas pedal as Gunnar darted into the darkness.

CHAPTER EIGHTEEN

As Damien sped toward High Noon Boulevard, I twisted around so I could look out the back window. Mama was right behind us, probably wondering what in the world was going on. I thought about calling her to explain, but I didn't want to distract her when she was driving so fast.

We had to park two streets away from the bakery, and although I couldn't see any flames from the direction of it, I could smell the smoke.

"I'll take Felipe and keep him away from everything," Vivian said as we scrambled out.

I rushed back to Mama's car. She was climbing out of the driver's seat as quickly as she could, a worried expression on her face and the six-shooter box forgotten on the back seat. Nick was already out of the car, and he said simply, "I smell smoke."

"Gunnar said the bakery is on fire," I explained quickly. "Let's get over there."

Damien and Lucy were waiting for us, but I waved them ahead. "We'll catch up!"

We weren't the only ones who wanted to see what was happening at the bakery. By the time we made it over to High Noon Boulevard, a small crowd had gathered. It looked like a mix of tourists and locals, and everyone was buzzing as they watched the firefighters coming and going from the front door of Bake in the Day.

The red fire truck looked so out of place on the Wild West street, but I was more interested in the firefighters themselves. They didn't look overly worried and were moving at a quick but not frantic pace.

"What's happening?" I asked Damien as I joined the throng.

"I just heard a man say the fire was in the back, where a piece of the building juts out into the alley."

"The kitchen expansion," Mama said. "Was there an accidental fire in the kitchen, or is the killer trying to erase evidence?"

"Jack was killed in the front part of the bakery, just past the windows here," I pointed out. "There shouldn't be any evidence in the kitchen."

Mama crossed her arms. "Even still, I can't imagine this fire was accidental. It would be an awfully big coincidence."

"But if it is arson, then who set the fire, and why?" I asked. "And is it the same person who set the general store on fire? Jack owned both properties, so maybe the fires are related to the murder, but how? And also—"

My laundry list of questions had to wait, because Chelsea and Sid were running toward us. Chelsea was crying hysterically. Sid, on the other hand, looked angry.

Behind the two of them was Quinn, looking just as uncomfortable as he had at the coffee shop earlier that day. His hunched shoulders suggested he wanted to be anywhere else in the world but right there in the middle of the drama.

"Mama! Olivia!" Chelsea stopped to let out a sob. "My bakery!"

Mama put a hand on Chelsea's arm and said soothing words while my eyes scanned the crowd. I spotted Fred, who had probably been wrapping up his day at the general store. I wondered if he was having a sense of déjà vu.

Fred had accused Sid of murdering Jack, then implied to me that he thought Sid had also set the fire at the general store. Who, then, did Fred think had started the bakery fire? Sid was unlikely to set his girlfriend's business ablaze.

A man walked past our group, a stunned look on his face. It was Ellis. "Oh, no. No. Not another fire," he moaned. He ran a hand through his hair. "These buildings are irreplaceable!"

"So glad he's worried about the people who work inside these places," Damien said to me.

"Ellis is thinking like someone who manages one of these historic buildings." I was trying to give him some grace, but I also thought it was a little tactless of Ellis to not ask if Chelsea was safe before lamenting the damage to the building.

Chelsea, at least, was calming down, so I asked her if she had been inside when the blaze started.

"No." Chelsea rubbed her hands over her eyes. "I close at three, since I'm usually out of most things by that time of day. Sid and I just happened to be at the saloon this evening, so I ran outside when I heard the sirens. I didn't think I'd find my own bakery on fire."

"I came back from the bathroom and had no idea where you were," Sid said. "The bartender said you ran out of the saloon like it was your house that was on fire. She had no idea how close to the truth that was."

Maybe Ellis sensed he was misplacing his priorities, because he stepped closer to our group and looked at Chelsea sympathetically. "The historic society can host a fundraiser. We'll help get the place fixed, and maybe you can have an even nicer kitchen than you had before."

Chelsea gave Ellis a shaky smile. "That's sweet of you,

but it's really a discussion you should be having with the owner of this building."

"Who's dead," Sid intoned.

"It will all get sorted out," Mama said, trying to sound reassuring.

As if to prove her statement, a firefighter walked up just then. "Chelsea Gentry? This is your bakery? You'll be happy to know the fire didn't get far. We caught it before a lot of damage could be done."

"Thank you. Honestly, it looks fine from out here," Chelsea said.

"The backside of the building took the brunt of it. Looks like the fire started just inside the window that looks out over the alley."

Damien and I exchanged a glance. The general store fire had been started in a window there, and it seemed the bakery fire had a similar origin.

I figured the fire department would be working with the police, and sure enough, I spotted Luis Reyes talking to a couple of firefighters closer to the bakery. Reyes was waving an arm toward the front door, and I wondered if the whole bakery would wind up festooned with crime scene tape. First, there had been a murder in the front of the shop, and then there had been a fire set in the back.

Is this all about Jack, or is Chelsea in danger?

After the firefighter had walked away, I gave Damien a quizzical look. "Who will be responsible for repairing the general store and the bakery? Or will these buildings go up for sale in their damaged states?"

"I have no idea. Maybe our buddy Leland Porter will buy them and fix them up. He's been talking about renovations to every place he wants to get his hands on, so the fires give him a head start in that department."

I sucked in my breath. "Maybe he set the fires himself!"

"I wouldn't rule him out. He'd get a cheaper price

because of the damage." Damien waved a hand toward the bakery. "I hope he does buy this place. Then he can stop pestering me about the Sanctuary."

I got the distinct feeling someone was looking at me, and I turned my head to see Reyes walking toward us. He had a wary expression as he said, "Olivia, are you here as a bystander, or are you searching for a killer?"

"We heard the bakery was on fire and came to see how bad it was." I gestured toward Chelsea. "Mama and Chelsea go way back."

Reyes nodded, then glanced around. "Is Justine with you?"

"No, she's at work, but I can tell her you said hi."

Reyes ducked his head slightly. I had never seen him look shy before. "That's okay. I'll call and tell her myself once she gets off work tonight."

"Speaking of work," Damien said, "it's time for us to get back there."

I glanced at my watch. "How is it only eight thirty?"

"I'm staying here for a while, so I can chat with some folks," Mama said. She gave Damien and me a wink, and this time, I didn't have to wonder what it meant. She was going to be collecting all the gossip and clues she could. "Come to the office in the morning, and I'll fill you both in."

It was a little after nine o'clock by the time I joined Theo and Seraphina in the lagoon vignette. There was a steady stream of guests, though, so I didn't have a chance to fill the two of them in on our wild night until the Sanctuary closed, and the last people had left the lagoon, screaming.

Theo turned his head away and sniffed loudly when I told them about seeing Lucille's ghost. I reached out and gave his hand a squeeze.

"Sorry," Theo said, wiping at his cheek with his free hand. "I wish I could have seen her."

"You will, soon," I promised.

"She really made me feel at home when I came to the Sanctuary. My mood was pretty low after I left the vampire enclave in North Carolina, and Lucille welcomed me here like I was family."

"I wish I could have met her," Seraphina said. "Fiona and I have only heard stories from you longtime Sanctuary folks."

The sentiment of those two was being expressed all over the Sanctuary. Word had already gone around that Lucille's ghost was getting stronger, and those who had known her were especially excited. I went home feeling hopeful.

On Sunday morning, Damien and I converged on the motel office at the same time. I had brought a cup of coffee with me, and I raised it in a little hello before we went inside to talk to Mama.

"I sure wish we had a box of cinnamon rolls to share while I tell you what happened after you left." Mama looked wistfully at a box of store-bought powdered-sugar donuts. "These just aren't the same."

"You have some gossip for us, then," I said, resting both elbows on the countertop.

"Leland Porter showed up just as the fire truck was leaving," Mama began.

"Also known as suspect number one," I said, looking significantly at Damien. "Maybe he came back to see how well his fire had done. Don't arsonists often return to the scene of the crime to survey their handiwork?"

"Even if he did set the fires," Mama continued, "he showed up for a different reason. He loudly asked where he could find the real estate agent representing all of Jack

Wiley's properties, because he was willing to buy all of them, in cash, right then and there."

CHAPTER NINETEEN

"I said Leland might buy up Jack's properties, but I didn't expect him to act that fast," Damien said. "He could at least have waited for the bakery to stop smoking."

"Maybe Leland really did set the fires to drive down the prices on both the general store and the bakery." While I pondered that, I absently grabbed a donut and bit into it. I screwed up my face after I swallowed. "Oh, no, this is nowhere near as good as Chelsea's cinnamon rolls."

"I told you," Mama said. "Anyway, why would Leland care about the prices of those buildings? The guy is loaded."

"He talks like he's trying to buy half of Nightmare," Damien said. "Maybe he needs to save money where he can."

I shook my head. "Setting fire to those places was risky. If the fire department hadn't shown up so fast last night, there would have been no bakery to buy."

"Then Leland could have moved on to thinking about the motel he wants to buy." Mama tapped a fingernail on the countertop. "We're meeting him at two o'clock tomorrow afternoon. Be here at the office by fifteen 'til, and I'll drive."

"Did you arrange the meeting when you saw him last night?" I asked.

"I pretended I was eager to talk, since I'd just heard him offer to buy a handful of other places. I told him I didn't want the motel to be left out!" Mama looked proud of herself.

"I'll be ready," I promised. "He's more of a suspect than ever now, after the fires and his very public cash offer. I wonder if anyone can tell me who called the fire department for both the general store and the bakery. If Leland set them, he would want to ensure they were put out before they grew out of control. Maybe he reported the fires himself."

"It's an interesting theory, but I don't think you can waltz into the city offices and ask for nine-one-one tapes," Damien said.

"I could waltz right into Reyes's office and ask, or have Justine ask him."

"Don't make that poor girl wring case information out of her boyfriend." Mama narrowed her eyes at me. "She's got her hands full trying to make him comfortable with the supernatural world."

Mama had a good point. As eager as friends like Justine and Clara were to help me solve this murder, I didn't want to put any strain on the relationship between Justine and Reyes. The two of them had barely started dating when he learned about the existence of ghouls, and Justine was already worried it would become too much for him.

"The good news in all of this," Damien said, "is that it's looking less and less likely that Chelsea killed Jack."

"I never thought she killed him," Mama said in a defensive tone.

"But the police probably did," I noted.

"And, now, they've got a list of other people who seem more likely." Mama was nodding. "Besides, why would

Chelsea set fire to her own bakery? She was having to take a hiatus while the place was a crime scene, but who knows when she'll be back up and running after this? Poor thing. She's going to be stressing out even more about money."

"Maybe she can bake some things out of her home kitchen, or find a temporary location," I said hopefully. I clamped a hand over my belly as it growled. "Talking about Chelsea's baking is making me hungry."

"Then let's go to lunch at the one place where you might catch some good gossip." Damien took my hand, but we didn't leave until Mama made us promise, twice, to share anything we might learn.

Damien and I walked to The Lusty Lunch Counter, taking a route that went right down High Noon Boulevard. Ordinarily, we would have avoided spending a lot of time on that street, since it got so jammed with tourists, but I had suggested taking a walk past the general store and the bakery, just in case there was anything interesting to see.

There wasn't. The general store still had the plastic tarp over the window, and the bakery looked perfectly ordinary from the High Noon Boulevard side. I was tempted to circle around to the back of the building to see what the damage looked like from the alley, but at the same time, I doubted I would learn anything by doing that.

Going all the way to the bakery had been slightly out of our way, but it was such a nice day out that I didn't mind the walk. I had my boyfriend by my side, the sun was shining, and everywhere I looked, tourists were smiling and taking photos.

Why can't every day in Nightmare be this relaxing?

The Lusty Lunch Counter was one street over from High Noon Boulevard. Despite being so close to Nightmare's hub of tourist activity, the atmosphere on that street was distinctly different. The old buildings were shabbier, and they housed local businesses rather than shops and restaurants designed to draw in tourists. The street hadn't been covered with dirt, and cars were parked on either side of it. There were no boardwalks, either.

The street didn't have the charm of High Noon Boulevard, but it looked authentic. It was a place where ordinary townspeople lived and worked, and, in the case of The Lusty, ate. Most of the white paint had peeled off the wooden clapboard building that housed the diner, and it was funny to think the place had probably looked a lot classier back when it was a mining-town brothel.

Damien and I found two stools at the stainless steel counter inside the diner, and I waved at my usual server, Ella. She was pouring coffee for someone a few stools over, and when her eyes met mine, they widened.

"She's going to have some interesting news for us," I told Damien.

"How do you know?"

"She's got that look on her face."

Damien chuckled and slid an arm around my shoulders. "You've become quite the local, haven't you? You run into someone you know everywhere we go."

"That's what happens when you're nosy and constantly get embroiled in murder investigations." I said it jokingly, but Damien's comment had made me feel happy. I hadn't even been in Nightmare for a full year, but I really was settling in nicely.

Damien got a thoughtful expression on his face. Quietly, he said, "We're going to practice your conjuring and my supernatural skills soon. We've been slacking lately."

"Have we?" I rotated on my stool so I could get a better look at Damien. "I think our combined power is what helped Lucille appear to Lucy during her session with Vivian. Our presence at the energy spring probably helped

136

her, too. I wonder if we're both exerting our power without even realizing it."

Damien gave me a searching look. "There was a time when you thought you were conjuring subconsciously, and that terrified you because you worried you were somehow causing all the murders in Nightmare."

"That's true. Since then, though, I've become more confident in my abilities. I understand them better, too."

"Let's put it to the test, then. What do you want most right now? Tell me, but don't focus on it, like you normally do when you're conjuring."

"I want Ella's news to paint a clear path to Jack's killer."

There was motion in my peripheral vision, and I looked up to see Ella. She leaned over the counter, her long brown ponytail sliding over her shoulders. "Hey, you two. I'll take your order, but first, what do you know about these fires?"

"Not much," I admitted. "I have some wild theories about them, but we don't know who could have set them, or why."

Ella's face was strained as she glanced in the direction of the door that led to the kitchen. "Jeff is so worried. He thinks we might be next."

"Why would he think that?" Damien asked. I couldn't figure out why the diner's manager would be concerned, either.

Ella spread her hands on the counter. "Someone is setting historic buildings on fire. We're in one of the oldest places in Nightmare."

"No," I said, putting a comforting hand over Ella's. "Jeff has nothing to worry about. Someone is setting buildings that were owned by Jack Wiley on fire. The Lusty isn't in danger."

Ella's eyes were even wider than they had been when

we first came into the diner. "You don't know, do you? There was another fire, early this morning."

"Was it one of the buildings Jeff owned in the New Downtown?"

"No. Someone set the Nightmare Grand on fire."

CHAPTER TWENTY

My mouth fell open, and to anyone who might have seen me in that moment, it probably looked comical. "That beautiful hotel?" I asked. "Was anyone hurt?"

"Everyone was fine, though I heard a few of the hotel's guests in here earlier, complaining about having to evacuate before dawn." Ella clicked her tongue. "As if having to stand around in your pajamas is worse than your hotel being on fire."

"What is the link between the fires?" Damien mused.

"And no wonder Jeff is worried." The Lusty's manager wasn't exactly a friend of mine, but we got along fairly well, and I didn't like thinking of him wondering if his diner might be next on the arson's list. "Ella, is he going to step up security here?"

Ella smiled wryly. "He says he's going to bring a blanket and pillow and sleep in his office."

"After we eat, we'll head to the Grand and see how bad the damage is," I said sadly.

"Oh, it's not bad," Ella assured me. "The fire was put out fairly quickly, from what I've heard. There's this area at the back of the hotel that's used for the employee entrance, food deliveries, and that kind of stuff. Well, they take the trash out there, too, and the fire was set inside a dumpster that sits near the back door. Someone was in here, claiming the flames were as high as the second-story windows."

"It must have been a smelly fire," I said, wrinkling my nose.

"Yuck, I hadn't thought of that. Anyway, what can I get for you two? Olivia, I assume you want a cheeseburger?"

"You know our local resident so well," Damien said, giving me a teasing nudge.

"It could be a coincidence," I pointed out after we had given Ella our orders. "Maybe this fire isn't related to the other two. Someone could have dropped a lit cigarette into the dumpster, or, I don't know, maybe the trash spontaneously combusted."

"I don't think that's how trash works." Damien laughed, then quickly sobered. "These fires have all been set after dark. If nothing else has been lit on fire by the time the Sanctuary closes for the night, I think we should put together a patrol."

"What would we even look for?"

"I'm not sure. But if Jeff's theory that historic properties are being targeted is correct, then we need a team keeping watch on the Sanctuary, too. The rest of us can go keep an eye on some of Nightmare's other notable buildings."

"The rest of us, except Mori. I think we should send her out for some fine dining."

Damien pretended he was gagging. "Can you imagine putting your lips on Leland's neck? Disgusting."

"Luckily, you're not a vampire. If Mori is keeping an eye on Leland, and someone does set a fire during the night, we'll be able to rule him out as our arsonist."

"I would ask what you'll be doing this afternoon, but I already know the answer is napping."

"You are absolutely correct. If we have guard duty

tonight, then I'm going to sleep as much as I can, while I can."

After eating our lunch, I thanked Ella for her intel and asked her to pass along my well-wishes to Jeff. We walked straight to the Nightmare Grand and followed the narrow lane that led to the back of the building.

The blackened dumpster was impossible to miss. It had been dragged into the middle of the lane, and it sat there, looking strangely forlorn. The backside of the building had also caught fire, which I was certain had been the arsonist's plan. The wall and roofline next to the back door were charred and crumbling, and some of the roof tiles were missing.

Despite Ella's assurances that the fire hadn't done extensive damage, I was still relieved to see for myself that things weren't so bad at the Nightmare Grand. It was nice being able to lay down for a nap without that worry hanging over my head. Instead, I was worried about what would happen after the sun went down that night. Like Damien, I was concerned someone might try to hurt the Sanctuary, too.

I enjoyed my very lazy afternoon. Even though I wound up not sleeping much, I felt rested after curling up with a book for a while. When I pulled on my Sanctuary hoodie before leaving for work, I felt ready for whatever the night might have in store for us.

First, though, I wanted to check in on Baxter. Damien had mentioned during lunch that the phoenix had grown even more, and when I walked into Damien's office, it was obvious at just a glance. Baxter didn't take up nearly the entire space inside the birdcage, like he had before he had burned into ash and become an egg, but he was quickly getting there.

"Are you coming to the family meeting?" I asked

Damien. He had been hunched over his laptop when I walked in, and he shut it with a satisfied snap.

"Yes. I spent the afternoon making a list of buildings I think are most likely to be targets for the arsonist. We'll assign everyone to a patrol area during the meeting, so as soon as we close tonight, everyone can head out and start the watch."

I smiled. "You had a much more productive afternoon than I did. Thank you for organizing all this."

Damien didn't look gratified. Instead, he said grimly, "I just got my father back. I'm not about to lose the Sanctuary."

Despite Damien's worry, I couldn't help my smile. "You talked about me being a local now, but look at you. You're doing everything in your power to keep the Sanctuary safe. When you first came back to Nightmare, you didn't feel quite so sentimental about it."

"It's not about the building itself." Damien stood and closed the distance between us so he could wrap his arms around me. "It's what's inside that matters."

"But it's a little bit about the building," I teased.

"Maybe a bit. This is home for a lot of people, and my father worked very hard to make it a comfortable place for the supernatural community. Besides, could you imagine having to rebuild the haunt in a different place? I can't think of anywhere in Nightmare that would be big enough."

"The Nightmare Grand, obviously," I said. "A haunted hotel attraction. The bravest of guests could stay overnight."

"I was thinking of taking over The Lusty Lunch Counter. A haunted brothel theme would really bring in the tourists."

Damien and I walked to the dining room, continuing to find ridiculous new locations and themes for Nightmare

Sanctuary Haunted House. It was fun because we knew it was something we wouldn't really have to do. The Sanctuary was going to be safe because we would protect it.

Justine sped through her announcements and assignments during the family meeting, giving Damien plenty of time to step up to the podium so he could fill everyone in on the fires and the patrol. It would make for a long night, since the groups wouldn't head out until after the Sanctuary closed at midnight, but no one complained. Instead, Malcolm and Gunnar both looked eager to participate, and Mori gave an uncharacteristic fist pump when Damien asked her if she'd mind looking after Leland Porter.

"Can I go with her?" Theo piped up. "I want to see if his blood is really as tasty as she says."

"You go find your own classy human," Mori said. "There are plenty of other guests at the Nightmare Grand who look like they're made of money."

"I wish my watch group was assigned to that area." Theo got a wistful look on his face, clearly thinking of the potential "snacks" he could have while keeping an eye out for the arsonist.

I would be working in the lagoon vignette that night, so as soon as Damien finished doling out patrol assignments, I hustled to the costume room so I could make a quick transformation into a pirate. I made it to the lagoon vignette just as the overhead lights blinked three times, then went out completely. The Sanctuary was open for business, and I had gotten to my usual spot just in time.

"There you are!" Seraphina called from her tank. "I wanted to tell you that Baxter is right on track in his growth. Since I'm babysitting him while the rest of you are on watch tonight, I'm going to read him some kids' books. I found a couple about monsters, so I thought he might enjoy those."

I tried to picture a siren reading children's stories to a phoenix, but it wasn't easy.

Work that night seemed to last twice as long as usual. Sunday night crowds were usually steady, though less chaotic than Friday and Saturday nights, so work should have sped past. I had plenty of guests to scare as they came through the lagoon vignette. However, I realized I was constantly on the lookout for Malcolm, Damien, or someone else who might show up at any moment to tell me there had been another fire.

The bakery fire had happened early on Saturday evening, which meant the arsonist wasn't waiting until really late, when they were less likely to be caught. The general store fire had happened much later, and the hotel fire had been set early in the morning, just before dawn.

It would be really nice if the arsonist could pick a time, so we'd know when to be on alert.

While I was pondering arsonist office hours, guests were streaming past, and I had to remind myself to be present. They deserved a good show—or a good scare—no matter what might be happening elsewhere in Nightmare at that moment.

Once the Sanctuary closed at midnight, I hurried to change back into my jeans and hoodie. I gave my hair a good shake to fluff it up, since it had been underneath my tricorn hat all night. Gunnar was the one cutting my hair since my arrival in Nightmare, and he was helping me keep it looking nice while I grew it out. I liked the longer look instead of the bob I'd had when I lived in Nashville.

Damien had instructed everyone to gather in front of the Sanctuary, so when I stepped outside, I found myself crammed under the portico with a small crowd of supernatural creatures. I sidled between Zach, Theo, and Fiona so I could reach the witches. "Good evening, ladies," I said.

"Let us hope it is," Morgan answered.

"No fires have yet been reported," Madge added, "so it is, for the moment, a good evening."

"And a good chance to wear my new socks." Maida lifted one leg so I could get a good look at a lacy pink sock, which was sticking out of her pointy-toed lace-up boot. The socks looked incredibly out of place with her high-necked black dress and black tights, but I could see they made Maida happy.

"Let me guess: Lucy helped you pick those out," I said.

Maida nodded emphatically.

"They look great. Pink is a good color on you."

"We'll see you later," Theo called to us. He and Fiona were leaving to take up their post near the general store.

"And we're off, too," Zach announced. He was teaming up with Malcolm to keep an eye on Cowboy's Corral. When Damien had mentioned it was on his list of historic places that might be under threat, Malcolm had insisted he be the one to guard it.

The witches were going to be keeping an eye on the old courthouse, which wasn't far from The Lusty Lunch Counter. Naturally, Damien and I were going to be guarding our favorite place to eat. We drove over to that part of town, then picked a street that would serve as the meeting point between the witches' patrol area and ours.

There was no one else out on the street at that late hour, so Damien and I slowly began walking in a loop that took us past both the front and rear of The Lusty. I wondered if Jeff really was inside, camping in his office.

I was just about to suggest to Damien that we call Jeff and let him know we were outside, so he wouldn't hear us and think we were there to cause trouble. I had only gotten the first few words out of my mouth, though, when Damien held up a hand to stop me.

"Someone's calling," he explained. He pulled out his

phone and answered it, putting it on speaker so I could hear, too. "Fiona, is everything okay?"

"Nothing is on fire, if that's what you mean." Fiona was speaking quietly but quickly. "What's the deal with the guy who runs the general store? He's out here in the alley behind the store, having what looks like a secret meeting with some younger man. It doesn't look like a friendly chat."

CHAPTER TWENTY-ONE

"If Fred is meeting someone in an alley in the middle of the night," I said, "it can't be good." I thought of my first week working at the Sanctuary, when I had followed Zach to a secret meeting in an alley, too. At the time, I'd thought Zach had murdered a local rancher, though I later found out his secret meeting was about something a lot less exciting. Accounting, in fact. "Fiona, what does the younger man look like?"

"Tall. Brown hair that needs to be tamed."

I gasped. "That sounds like Quinn!"

"Who?"

"Chelsea Gentry's son. It's entirely possible either he or Fred killed Jack, but what in the world are they doing together in the alley?"

"Stop wondering and get over here!" Fiona said. She sounded like she wanted to laugh at me.

"On our way," Damien said before putting his phone away.

It would only take us a couple minutes to walk to the area of the general store, and as we went, I began throwing out all the questions my mind could come up with. "Are Quinn and Fred working together? Is one of them the killer, and the other the arsonist? But why would either one of them torch their own stores? Well, the bakery doesn't belong to Quinn, but his mom owns it, and he works there. And are the two of them meeting now so they can set another fire? Or—Hold on, Damien. I have to catch my breath."

We had been hurrying, our pace just shy of a run, and as it turned out, I couldn't run both my legs and my mouth at the same time.

Damien slowed, and I shut my mouth. By the time we saw Fiona and Theo huddled behind a pickup truck parked in the alley behind the general store, I was breathing at a normal rate. We joined our friends in the shadow of the truck, and when I peeked around the tailgate, I spotted Fred and Quinn a short distance away. I could hear their voices but couldn't make out the words. Still, the angry gestures indicated it was a contentious conversation.

"I wish we could eavesdrop," I whispered.

Theo pointed to the shadows to the left of where Fred and Quinn were standing. "We are."

I squinted, and I could just barely make out the lines of a tall hat and a form that was slightly darker than its surroundings. "Is that Malcolm? But he's at Cowboy's Corral tonight."

"Theo texted him while I was on the phone with you two," Fiona said. "Malcolm knew we'd need his heightened hearing to find out what this meeting is about."

That meant Malcolm had made the trip from the motel to the alley in just a few minutes. I knew he was fast, but I hadn't realized he was *that* fast. I suppressed a shudder as my mind returned to Malcolm's pep talk for Lucy. I wondered how many people he had hunted down before he had mastered control of his wendigo instincts, and just how much time and patience it had taken him to act like a human again.

It was another ten minutes before Fred and Quinn

wrapped up their discussion. Quinn headed in the opposite direction from us, but Fred turned and moved toward our hiding spot.

"Is this his truck?" Damien hissed.

"The recycling bins! Go!" Fiona gave me a shove in the direction of the blue bins lined up near the back of the general store.

The four of us crouched down in the tiny space behind the bins. Damien was pressed up against my left side while Theo was on my right. I felt slightly claustrophobic, but it was better than getting caught spying on Fred. I ducked my head when he started the truck and the headlights came on, flooding the alley with light, but thankfully, we were still in the darkness in our hiding spot.

I didn't let out the breath I was holding until the truck's taillights disappeared as Fred turned right out of the alley. "That was close."

"That was fun!"

I looked over to see Theo grinning.

Damien offered me a hand, and I stood slowly. My knees weren't happy about the crouching down.

Malcolm was coming our way, and we eagerly grouped around him, anxious to know what he'd learned.

"They're both scared," Malcolm began. "I'm not sure why they were meeting here in the first place, since none of us heard the beginning of the conversation, but I got here just in time to know they feel like these fires are personal. Both men agreed that if Jack Wiley was still alive, they'd think the fires were some kind of revenge on him."

"That makes sense," I said. "People were unhappy with Jack, so they might go after the places he made his money from."

"Except he was murdered, so these fires aren't about Jack," Damien noted.

"That's the conclusion Fred and Quinn came to, as

well." Malcolm looked at me. "I can't imagine the nice woman who runs the bakery has a lot of enemies, but Fred and Quinn feel like the fires are some kind of retaliation against the renters themselves."

"Whether or not someone is setting the fires for revenge, it sounds like neither Fred nor Quinn is the arsonist." I frowned. "If, of course, both of them were being honest about their suspicions. Plus, one of them could still be the killer."

Malcolm turned to look down the alley, in the direction Quinn had gone. "I think that's a fair assessment. I'm happy to tail him."

"I doubt he's going anywhere but home," Fiona said. "Whatever those two were up to, it's over. But I would really like to know why they were meeting in the middle of the night to begin with."

Theo slung an arm around my neck and gave me a look that was part pride and part teasing. "Knowing Olivia, she'll just drop into the general store tomorrow and ask Fred point-blank what he was doing."

"I agree with Fiona," Damien said. "Those two aren't worth tailing. Let's all head back to our patrol areas, in case other people are running around Nightmare in the middle of the night."

Damien's phone buzzed, and the bright screen illuminated his face as he read the text message he had just gotten. He laughed softly. "If we catch anyone running around, it won't be Leland Porter. Mori says he's fast asleep in his hotel room, and she thinks she mesmerized him so that he won't wake up until his alarm clock goes off in the morning."

"Well done, Mori," I murmured.

We split up, with Malcolm heading back to Cowboy's Corral while Damien and I returned to our section of the historic district. We stopped along the way to fill in the witches, who said they hadn't seen anyone except a drunk tourist wobbling his way back to a bed and breakfast not far from The Lusty Lunch Counter.

After another two hours of walking in circles, I was barely able to keep my eyes open. So, it was with blurry vision that I spotted someone rushing toward us as we rounded the corner on the far edge of our circuit. I was wide awake in an instant, and I grabbed Damien's arm.

It was only after a jolt of adrenaline had started coursing through my body that I realized it was Mori, and she wasn't running but simply moving with her supernatural speed. "Oh, good, it's just a vampire," I said with a shaky laugh.

Mori grimaced as she came to a stop in front of us. "Sorry. Did I scare you?"

I pressed a hand against my heart. "I should be thanking you, because I needed something to wake me up. That was better than a whole pot of coffee."

"Leland is still fast asleep, so I figured it was safe to leave him."

"Did you sit there and watch him sleep for two hours?"

Mori nodded. "A little creepy, right? I felt like some kind of weird stalker. Since he's down for the count, though, I thought I'd volunteer to patrol. Why don't you two head home?"

I didn't argue, especially when Mori added she had slept all day, so she had no problem circling the historic buildings until dawn. Damien drove me home, and I flopped into bed without even changing into my pajamas.

I regretted my decision when I woke up on Monday morning. My pirate makeup, which was much more dramatic than my everyday look, had smeared across my face and the pillowcase. My hair was a tangled mess, and I had the first twinge of a cramp in my left calf.

Of course, the cramp had nothing to do with skipping

my bedtime routine and everything to do with walking in circles for hours.

Mama had said I needed to be at the motel office by one forty-five so we could drive to our meeting with Leland Porter. That meant I had time to catch up on some normal, everyday stuff, like grocery shopping. I bought a bunch of bananas when I went, hoping the potassium would help with my still-tender calf.

My wardrobe in Nightmare was vastly different than it had been in Nashville, when I had worn business attire nearly every day, often with a designer label. But I still had a few pieces from that old life, and I chose a smart navy-blue dress for the meeting with Leland. The color looked great with my auburn hair. I even had one last pair of stockings in my possession, and I put those on along with low red heels.

I knew I had chosen my outfit well when I walked into the office and spotted Damien, who greeted me with, "Wow."

"Thanks. Are you going with us?"

"No. I'm going to keep an eye on things here for Mama. I even brought my father with me." Damien nodded toward the birdcage sitting on the countertop.

Mama and Benny came down the stairs just then, and they were both dressed nicely, as well. Mama had put on a flowing denim skirt that went all the way to her ankles, and her white blouse had a Western look. Benny was in khaki pants and a blue Oxford shirt.

"You two look nice," I commented.

"Susie always looks nice," Benny said, beaming at his wife. "The three of us will look like real motel moguls when we walk into the meeting."

Mama raised a finger. "Remember, Benny, we're not actually selling Cowboy's Corral."

"Well, if he offers us a couple million…"

"No!"

Mama drove, with Benny beside her and me squeezed into the back seat of the old Mustang. We were meeting Leland at a cafe in the New Downtown. It was a place I hadn't visited yet, but I'd heard locals mention it. It was impossible to forget a name like Vines and Vittles.

The cafe was a bright, welcoming space with booths lining both sides of the long room. Planters hung from the exposed wooden rafters above us, and some of the trailing vines reached down nearly to the top of my head.

Leland was already there, and he stood to shake hands with Mama and Benny before sitting back down. I slid onto the bench next to him, figuring he and I had seen each other so much lately that we were well past the hand-shaking phase.

After some small talk, Mama got down to business. "I'm glad you're still interested in buying Cowboy's Corral, Mr. Porter."

Leland frowned. "The way places around this town keep catching on fire, maybe I don't want to own anything."

"Do you think the fires were someone's way of trying to scare you off?" I asked.

"Scare me?" Leland made a scoffing noise. "Not just that. Someone in this town is trying to hurt me."

CHAPTER TWENTY-TWO

"Why do you think someone is trying to hurt you, Mr. Porter?" Mama asked.

"And no one was around when those fires were set," I added. "You weren't in danger."

"Yes, I was," Leland retorted. "Someone set a fire at my hotel, and I had to evacuate my room along with everyone else. It's more than just the fires, though."

Leland fell silent and shifted his eyes upward. He seemed relieved when someone came over right then to ask what we'd like to order. Once the server was gone, though, he continued to stare at the trailing vines overhead.

"You can tell us," I said gently. "What else has happened?"

"I think someone drugged me last night."

It was odd to see Leland looking so uncomfortable. The pretentious smirk he usually had on his face was gone.

Benny leaned as far over the table as he could. "If that's true, you need to tell the police."

"I did. I reported the attack to them this morning."

I had a horrible sinking feeling. "What makes you think you were drugged?"

"I was at the saloon last night, and I only have fuzzy memories of it. I don't remember leaving, and I woke up this morning still fully dressed. But I swear, I only had one whiskey." Leland hesitated, then tugged at the collar of his crisp white shirt. "Plus, there's this."

There were two small red dots on Leland's neck, about an inch apart from each other.

I wasn't surprised. I hadn't initially connected Leland's suspicion he was drugged and Mori's mesmerizing, but it had clicked when Leland had called it an attack. I wondered if Reyes had seen the report, and if he had figured it out, as well.

"I think someone injected me with something," Leland concluded.

Mama's eyes flicked to mine, and I knew she was thinking the same thing I was. "Maybe you had more drinks at the saloon than you thought," she said. "Plus, the stress you're under right now might have added to that foggy feeling."

"Then explain my neck!"

"Sand fleas, probably," Mama said, her face perfectly straight. I, on the other hand, had to clamp my lips together to keep from smiling.

Leland jutted out his chin defiantly. "If this is all meant to hurt me or scare me, they'll have to try harder. The dumpster fire at the hotel was close to the room I'm staying in, and even that won't scare me off."

Could that be the connection to the fires? They were all set to warn Leland away?

"It seems to me the arsonist is doing you a favor," Benny said. "The more those places are damaged, the cheaper they'll be."

"The damage will still have to be repaired, though," Mama pointed out.

Leland waved a hand. "That doesn't matter. If I can get the general store and the bakery, I'll be renovating both. It won't cost me any more money now than it would have before those places were damaged."

Again, I had to wonder if Leland had set the fires himself. If he was planning extensive renovations, like he had hinted at for the Sanctuary, then a little fire damage wouldn't even matter. He could have set the fire at the Nightmare Grand to make it look like he was being targeted, so he would fall off the list of arsonist suspects.

"Would you be renovating Cowboy's Corral if you buy it?" Mama asked.

"The neon sign out front could use an overhaul." When Mama looked like she was going to protest, Leland added, "That sign is a part of American road-trip history. I would refurbish it, not get rid of it."

Mama's shoulders relaxed, and she leaned back. Again, I had to keep myself from smiling. This entire discussion about selling the motel was a farce, but she seemed to have forgotten that for a moment.

Either that, or she was doing a fine bit of acting.

Leland said he would need to make a thorough tour of the motel before he could say anything more about what he might want to do with the place, so after we'd all had coffee and chatted about the strong tourism industry in Nightmare, we wrapped up our meeting.

On the drive back to the motel, Benny craned his head toward my spot in the back seat. "Did our fake meeting help?"

"It helped Leland look more like the arsonist than ever." I told him and Mama my theory that he had set the fires himself, adding the Nightmare Grand to the list to make it look like he was the victim rather than the arsonist.

"Every place he wants to buy is historic," Mama pointed out. "Maybe he's vying for the Grand, too, even though it's not for sale. If he could scare the owners, or make them feel like repairs would be outside their budget, he could jump in and buy the place."

"Let's say that's true," I said. "Even if Leland is the

157

arsonist, is he also the killer? Did he kill Jack to force a sale of those buildings? Or is he simply taking advantage of the opportunity the murderer created?"

"I guess we'll have to schedule another meeting to find out." I could see Mama's smile in the rearview mirror.

All three of us were surprised when we pulled into the motel's drive and saw Nick's tow truck parked in front of the office. I worried the unexpected visit meant something was wrong, but Mama was calm as she announced, "This has to do with Lucy."

"How do you know?" Benny asked.

Mama made a humming noise. "With all the psychic growth Lucy is experiencing, I think it's affecting me, too. As her abilities grow, mine are getting pulled along, too. It happened with Lucille, when we were kids. Back then, I focused on shutting off that part of myself. Now that I'm older and not self-conscious about being different than my peers… Why not see where it all goes?"

Benny waved his hands in the air, like he was seeing a sign in his mind's eye. "Free psychic reading with every room reservation! Soft beds and talkative spirits!"

When we trooped into the office, Benny was still coming up with taglines for a combination motel and psychic-reading business. "Color TV and even more colorful séances!"

Nick and Damien were standing at the countertop, deep in conversation, while Lucy was sitting in a chair with a book on her lap. All three of them looked at us with raised eyebrows.

"Benny is trying to find a new angle for the motel," Mama explained.

"Who needs a séance when you've got the school play-ground?" Nick said. He waved an arm toward Lucy, the sleeve of his white overalls peppered with oil stains. "Lucy saw the ghost again today."

"I saw all of them today," Lucy clarified. She put her book aside and hopped up. "The girl I always see was there, and I talked to her, but the other two didn't say anything. They weren't as bright as Hazel."

"You learned her name?" I asked.

"Their names were in that old newspaper story you gave me, and I said each name until she nodded. And then I said, 'My great-aunt Lucille said I should talk to you and ask what you need.' And then, she talked!"

"That's fantastic, Lucy!" Mama was beaming at her granddaughter. "Lucille is going to be so proud of you. What did Hazel say?"

"She said they found him."

I gasped. "Found who? The person responsible for their disappearance?" The case of the Vanishing Girls, as they were known, had never been solved. The three girls had gone missing after school one day in the nineteen fifties, and no trace of them had ever been found.

Lucy nodded. "Yeah. Hazel said a man took them in his car after school. They got in the car because he said they'd go get ice cream, but that's not what happened."

I knew my face must have been as pale as Mama's as she made a go-ahead motion with her hand. "What really happened?" Mama asked.

"He gave them cupcakes to eat while he drove toward the ice cream parlor, but they tasted bad, and the girls died." Lucy said it so simply, and I wondered if she really understood what she had just told us, or how important it was to finally get answers about the long-lost girls. "They never got the ice cream he had promised them."

"Poisoned," Benny said under his breath. "What a monster."

"Did Hazel tell you who did this to them?" I asked. *And,* I added to myself, *why?* Like Benny had just said, the man must have been a monster.

"She said they found him, but he's dead, too."

"If they found him," I pressed, "then they must have learned his name. What he did is an awful crime, and even if he's dead, it's important to know the truth."

Lucy shrugged. "I asked what his name was, but Hazel said it doesn't matter. She told me it's history now, and the living can't help."

CHAPTER TWENTY-THREE

"Those poor girls." Mama shook her head sadly.

"Lucy." I took a step toward her. "Hazel told you the living can't help them get resolution. Can the dead help?" I was thinking of Lucille, or even Tanner and McCrory. Could ghosts confront other ghosts?

Lucy brightened. "Oh, that's a good question! I'll ask Hazel the next time I see her. Maybe the funny cowboys could help."

I laughed. "You're reading my mind."

"Ooh, is that something I can do now?"

"It's just a saying. Right?" I looked at Mama, who shrugged. She didn't know if Lucy's psychic abilities included clairvoyance, either.

"Miss Vivian can help, too, maybe. I'll bet she has lots of ghosts she can ask." Lucy looked thoughtful for a moment, then sighed dramatically. "Okay, I have to get back to this book I'm reading for school."

As Lucy settled into the chair again, I looked around at the others. "She had a chat with a ghost about a horrific triple murder, and she's so unfazed by it."

"She's not daunted by the supernatural," Mama noted. "Lucille was always the same way. Absolutely fearless about things that would terrify the rest of us."

"Speaking of fearless," Damien said, "Olivia, would

you like to scare people this evening? I know Monday is your day off, but Clara won't be working tonight."

"Of course I can fill in for her, but is Clara okay?"

"If you ask her, she'll tell you she's at death's door, but she's going to be just fine. She was patrolling around the Sanctuary last night, and she heard a noise in the underbrush. She thought it might be the arsonist, coming to set the place on fire, so she bravely took off toward the sound."

I crossed my arms. "I take it the sound was not made by the arsonist."

"No. It was a small deer. Clara learned this only after she had bumped into a beehive."

Mama, Benny, Nick, and I all gasped, but Damien looked calm. "She only got one sting, but it was right on the tip of her nose. Her not wanting to work tonight is more about her being self-conscious than how she feels."

"Maybe Morgan, Madge, and Maida can make something to help the swelling and redness," I suggested. I reminded myself not to say the words *witch* or *potion* in front of Nick.

"She's trying every remedy she can think of, but I told her to take the night off, anyway. We'll need her more once we close tonight."

"You want to keep up the watch," I guessed.

"Hopefully, no one sets fire to the motel," Mama said, looking around as if she might catch the arsonist in the act right then and there.

"We're keeping an eye on this place," Damien assured her. "Zach and Malcolm were patrolling around here last night, and they'll be here again tonight. We're all taking sections of town that have historic buildings."

That seemed to appease Mama. "I trust those two to keep this place safe. Now, you all get out of here. Damien and Olivia, you two need to get some rest if you're going to be up all night. Nick, take Lucy home and feed that child a treat. She's earned it. But please, don't give her a cupcake after that story she told us. Benny, you can stay here, with me."

We all promised to do just as Mama ordered, though Damien walked me back to my apartment before he went home. I filled him in on our meeting with Leland and my speculation that he was the arsonist.

"That would fit with last night's events," Damien said. "Mori put Leland to bed, and there were no fires."

"Poor Reyes must be wondering what we're up to, because there is no way he read Leland's report without realizing a vampire was involved."

"I'll ask Justine to call Luis and fill him in. He may not like it, but unless he's willing to become a vampire slayer, he's going to have to contend with the fact that Mori and Theo have to survive somehow."

"Luis has met Leland, so I doubt he'll be too upset about Mori snacking on him."

Normally, Monday was my version of a Saturday since it was my day off. Instead, I left for the Sanctuary early that night since I had agreed to fill in for Clara, and I wanted to see her before the family meeting. I found her in her apartment on the second floor. When she answered the door, she gestured at her nose. "Look how ugly I am!"

"You are not ugly. You look like you've had a cold, that's all."

"I look like Rudolph the Red-Nosed Reindeer!"

"Are all fairies this vain?" I asked. I didn't feel bad about teasing Clara in the slightest. No one would notice the bee sting on her nose, especially inside the haunt itself, where the lighting was low.

"Yes." Clara waved me inside and flopped down onto her sofa. "But it's not just the bee sting. I'm worried."

"About the fires?"

Clara grabbed a bowl of chocolate candies and sank a hand into them as I sat down next to her. Then, she seemed to feel she was being impolite, because she pulled her hand out and waved the bowl toward me. "You want some?"

I snickered. "No, I do not want candy you've had your fingers all over. Tell me what's got you worried."

"What if The Caffeinated Cadaver is next on the arsonist's list?" Clara's voice was timid. She wasn't thinking of the coffee shop itself. The historic building had once been where Nightmare's undertaker practiced, and while the ground floor was a coffee shop popular with tourists and locals alike, it was the bar in the basement Clara was thinking of. Her family had been running Under the Undertaker's for years.

"Theo and Fiona were patrolling that stretch of High Noon Boulevard last night," I said thoughtfully. "Why don't you take that area tonight? It might make you feel better if you're right there, so you know the bar is safe."

"And my family is keeping an eye out, too, so I can be close to them." Clara sat up straight and put aside the candy bowl. "Yeah, that's a good suggestion. In fact, I might go keep watch now, while the rest of you are working."

"Good plan."

Clara walked with me to Damien's office so she could tell him she wanted to patrol near her family's bar, then we headed to the dining room to let Justine know where she'd be that night. The whole time, Clara didn't mention the bee sting or how self-conscious she was about it. It had been her worry about her family's livelihood that had put her into such a miserable mood, and feeling like she could help had been all she needed to forget her vanity.

Normally, Clara either floated between scenes, filling in for people during their breaks, or she portrayed the fortune teller in the spooky cabin vignette. Vivian was going to be the fortune teller that night, which meant I would be the one floating between scenes.

I had felt a flare of panic when Justine announced that, since it was something I had never done before, but she assured me it would be a breeze.

For the first hour and a half, I merely helped out where needed backstage. I had thought that part of my evening would be easy, but I was wrong. There were a lot of things that could go wrong inside a haunted house attraction, as it turned out, especially when that attraction was housed in an old building. I soon learned where the fuse box was, since the cemetery vignette's lights kept tripping, and I had to run between the costume room and the haunt several times.

When I began giving people breaks, my pace was slightly less chaotic. I would throw on the barest of costumes for each vignette where I was filling in: a medical gown and cheap ratty wig for the hospital vignette, a long white dress and the same ratty wig for the cemetery—though I was downright boring compared to the show Fiona put on in that scene—and a black velvet wrap and plastic fangs for the hallway that looked like a mausoleum.

Once everyone had gotten their break for the night, Justine told me to go ahead and put on my pirate costume so I could spend the rest of the night in the lagoon vignette. It felt good to be in the same place, and the same clothes, for a while.

There were never a lot of guests on a Monday night, so I chatted with Theo and Seraphina in between groups. "How was your night of babysitting a phoenix?" I asked Seraphina.

"Baxter is a very well-behaved baby bird," she said. "In fact, he's a lot more mischievous as a full-grown man."

"Oh, so he's a troublemaker like Theo?" Just a few

seconds before, Theo had snuck up behind me and done his best impression of a zombie. I had threatened to dump him into Seraphina's tank if he tried it again.

"Baxter was the type of guy who would put a fake corpse in a vignette without telling anyone," Seraphina explained. "And he'd hide it somewhere, so you didn't spot it until you were right on top of it. He always said that since we're the ones who make people scream in fright, it was especially satisfying when he could make us scream instead."

"You say he was that type of guy, and he still is," Theo reminded her. "He's just taking a little hiatus from being a human right now."

"I can't wait until he's mature enough to transform. I've missed Baxter. He's always been a father figure to me." Seraphina glanced over her shoulder. "Oh, here we go!"

A couple had just come through the door into the lagoon. Seraphina dove under the water while Theo and I hurried to get back to our usual spots along the low boardwalk that stretched above the floor, which was designed to look like the surface of water. There were even a few shallow pools in the room to add to the effect.

As the couple got closer to me, I locked eyes with the woman and gave her my most menacing stare. Her hands were curled into fists and pressed against her mouth, a position she had assumed after Theo had made her shriek and take a jump backward.

My stare turned into one of surprise when I realized the woman was Rose, the hostess from the Nightmare Grand tearoom. She gave me a pleading look, and she bumped up against me as she and her companion passed by. One of her hands lowered, and I felt her fingers against my own as she pushed something small into my palm.

The second Rose had disappeared through the doorway to the next vignette, I looked down to see a small folded piece of paper. No one else was coming through, so I hollered to Theo, "I'll be right back!"

The door into the tunnels was cleverly hidden near the back end of the prop pirate ship, so it was virtually invisible to guests. I slipped out of the vignette and hurried through the tunnels until I was in a spot where I knew we stored a couple of flashlights.

I unfolded the piece of paper, then grabbed a flashlight and clicked it on. Once my eyes adjusted to its bright beam, I began to read Rose's note, which looked like it had been written in a hurry.

I'm sorry I didn't come when I said I would, Rose had written. *I got scared, but I know I have to be brave. I'll be outside the old bank at two o'clock in the morning. I need to tell you before he comes after me, too.*

CHAPTER TWENTY-FOUR

I hastily read through Rose's note again. Who was the *he* that she referenced? And why in the world did Rose feel like she was in danger?

Maybe she knew a lot more about what was going on than any of us had realized.

I folded the note slowly and thoughtfully before tucking it into one of the leather pouches hanging from my pirate belt. I would just have to wait until two o'clock to find out. I hoped, this time, Rose wouldn't bail on our plan. The fact that she was acting in such a clandestine manner showed just how frightened she was.

When I re-emerged into the lagoon vignette, a party of four was gaping at Seraphina, and I slid into place just in time to make two of them giggle nervously as they passed by.

The next time we had a break between guests, I hastily told Theo and Seraphina what had happened. They agreed it was ominous, and Theo offered to tag along as what he called "your personal vampire pirate bodyguard."

I told him thank you but that I doubted Rose would want someone she didn't know showing up with me.

Once the Sanctuary closed at midnight, I quickly changed out of my costume and went to Damien's office.

When I told him about Rose's note and request to meet, he immediately said he would come with me.

"I'm going to tell you the same thing I told Theo," I said. "Rose is already scared, and I'm afraid she might not tell me her news if I have anyone with me."

"Then she won't know anyone is with you. I'm going, and I'll grab a couple others to go, as well." Damien looked at me grimly. "If Rose is in danger, then you're also in danger by going to this meeting. We'll stay out of sight, and neither one of you will even know we're there."

I quickly agreed to that plan. I would feel safe, and Rose wouldn't get spooked.

With nearly two hours to wait before the meeting, I went to the dining room to see what my friends were up to. The witches were clustered around a table along with Fiona and Seraphina. Madge was laying out a board game.

"Want to play?" Fiona asked.

I was about to say yes, but instead, I said, "I'm going to hang back. I want to do some conjuring while I kill time."

Fiona nodded. "Seraphina told us about your tearoom informant. Conjuring is a good idea."

So, instead of joining the game or sitting down to chat with Gunnar, Zach, and Mori, I sat down at the table where Baxter's birdcage was sitting. He, I knew, would let me conjure in peace. "Hey, Baxter," I said, tapping my index finger against the bars of the cage. "You're so big!"

In fact, I realized, he looked almost as big as he had been before bursting into flames and being reduced to ashes.

I began to focus on how much I wanted Rose and myself to be safe and to have an informative meeting. With my eyes closed, I pictured her and myself standing in the darkness outside Nightmare's old bank, and I imagined

170

feeling the thrill of learning new details that would help us identify the killer and the arsonist.

It was Seraphina's voice that broke into my thoughts. "Olivia, does he look hungry? It's almost dinnertime."

I blinked my eyes open and looked at the phoenix. Baxter gazed at me serenely. "What does a hungry phoenix even look like?"

"He'll dip his head, and sometimes, he'll make a low cooing noise."

"In that case, he doesn't look hungry."

Fiona laughed heartily. "Sera, what are you going to do once Baxter is human again? You're enjoying taking care of him so much that we'll have to get you another bird!"

"Maybe a fish," Seraphina suggested. "Or even a whole school of them. They could perform with me in the lagoon vignette!"

A debate about whether fish could be trained to perform was breaking out as I closed my eyes and tuned out the chatter again.

Maybe I was deeply into my conjuring, or maybe I had fallen asleep, but in what seemed like no time at all, Damien was gently shaking my shoulder. "It's time," he told me.

I stretched my arms and stood up. "I wasn't sleeping, I swear."

"Sure," Theo said. He was standing at Damien's elbow, an excited look in his eyes. "I get to be your bodyguard tonight, after all."

"Me, too." Malcolm stepped up next to Theo and lifted his top hat. "Out of everyone at the Sanctuary, I'm the best at not being seen."

"Like when you got to listen in on Quinn and Fred having their discussion in the alley," I said. "It's nice that you're able to use your supernatural skills to solve crimes."

"It is nice." Malcolm patted his long black coat.

"Maybe I would look good in a Nightmare Police Department uniform."

"I can't imagine you in any color but black," I told him. "Besides, no one can make a coat swoop as dramatically as you do, and I don't think the police department issues coats as part of the uniform."

"I'll have to stick to my current career, then."

While I had been conjuring—or sleeping—Damien had been making a plan. He, Theo, and Malcolm had each chosen spots near the bank where they would be able to see Rose and me but still be hidden in the shadows. They would leave for the meeting before me, so by the time I showed up, the three of them would be in position.

It would only take me about five minutes to get to the old bank if I drove, but I had walked to work that night. When I pointed out the irony of being watched during the meeting but alone for the walk to High Noon Boulevard, Damien grinned proudly. "We already thought of that. Zach will be tailing you. I considered loaning you my car, but walking lets us all keep an eye out for the arsonist. We get to protect you and the town at the same time."

Damien, Theo, and Malcolm left a few minutes later. As soon as they were out the door, I went to Zach's office and told him to walk with me rather than somewhere behind me. "You can drop back when we get close to the bank," I told him.

Zach muttered something about having to be social, but he agreed to the plan. I figured a little small talk would be good for him, since he seemed to be in an especially grumpy mood that night.

As we walked toward High Noon Boulevard, I asked Zach how his girlfriend, Laura, was doing. That immediately lifted his mood, and he launched into a description of the fun antics they had gotten into during the most recent full moon. Zach had been lucky to find another werewolf who made him so happy.

When we were about three blocks from the bank, Zach wished me luck and stepped sideways into a shadowy alcove. I continued on, reminding myself that I was meeting the nice woman from the Nightmare Grand, not some villain.

Nevertheless, the words from Rose's note kept rising in my mind, and I realized it wasn't Rose that had me feeling jumpy but the idea that whoever was making Rose feel threatened might have followed her to the meeting.

But I have people following me, too, so it's okay.

The Nightmare Bank was a simple one-story wooden structure on High Noon Boulevard. It had been the first bank in the town, though a second one on the opposite end of Nightmare had soon followed. The story went that the bank was so popular with outlaws that wealth had been divided between the two locations. That way, if one bank got robbed, there was still plenty of money inside the other.

Tanner, of course, was one of those outlaws who had made a second bank necessary. He was very proud of that fact.

I didn't expect Rose to be standing on the boardwalk in front of the building, because there would be too much chance of someone spotting us. Instead, I headed down the narrow side street to the right of the bank.

Rose wasn't there, though as I walked, I heard Damien call softly, "Good luck!" I couldn't see him, but I gave a little wave in the general direction his voice had come from.

Rose wasn't behind the bank, either, so I kept walking until I was on the other side of the building. That street was even darker, and as I moved forward, I could just make out the form of someone standing with their back pressed up against the wooden siding.

"Rose?" I called softly.

"You came." Rose took two steps forward, then stopped and looked worriedly in both directions.

I decided being honest with her might be helpful. "I've got friends posted nearby. They're keeping an eye out, so you and I are both safe."

"Friends you trust?"

"I trust them with my life."

Rose didn't look convinced, and she grabbed my sleeve at the wrist and dragged me farther into the shadows.

"Is this about Ellis and Fred threatening Jack?" I asked.

"Yes. When we talked at the tearoom, I made it sound like I had gotten hints about it from working at the Grand with Ellis." Rose's face tilted downward, and she shifted uncomfortably. "That wasn't true. My friend Quinn actually saw what happened."

"Quinn," I repeated incredulously. "Chelsea Gentry's son."

"Yeah. He's a friend. Well, sometimes we go out, but he's not my boyfriend. I'm sorry I didn't tell you I heard the information from someone else."

"You were trying to protect Quinn," I guessed.

Rose nodded and finally lifted her eyes to meet mine again. "The police already talked to him about Jack's murder, because he's said some awful stuff about the guy. Jack wasn't a good stepfather to him."

"So I've heard."

"Quinn says he told the police about what he saw Ellis and Fred doing, but the police didn't seem to take him seriously. I thought you might look into it, if they won't."

I put a reassuring hand on Rose's arm. "I'm sure the police are looking into Quinn's claims. But it doesn't hurt to have more minds working on things. What did Quinn witness?"

"They weren't physically hurting Jack, but Quinn overheard the three of them talking one night, outside the saloon. Ellis and Fred were making all these threats to Jack, saying they would protest what he was doing to the city council and bring a lawsuit against him."

"For what?"

Rose shrugged. "Quinn said he didn't hear what it was all about. Just that Ellis and Fred were really laying into Jack. Quinn told me he wanted to go high-five Ellis and Fred for standing up to the guy, but after the murder, he worried that whatever they'd been talking about that night had led to one of them killing Jack."

"Ellis and Fred don't get along well," I said, more to myself than to Rose. I was thinking of Fred's display window at the general store that had made Ellis so indignant. "Why would they team up to go after Jack?"

Rose shrugged. "Maybe their shared dislike of Jack was stronger than their dislike of each other."

Maybe. Or, maybe, Quinn had fabricated the story to make himself look innocent. I just couldn't picture a scenario in which Fred and Ellis would go after Jack together. Separately? Sure. But not as a team.

There was something else about the story, too. "Their behavior certainly wasn't polite, but it doesn't make either one of them seem more guilty than anyone else. We know Fred was mad about the threats of a rent hike, and I think that makes him more suspicious than some complaint to city council."

"But they were threatening a lawsuit, too. And Quinn said Fred has been acting kind of shady since Jack died."

Which Quinn would know all about, since he and Fred had met secretly in the alley behind the general store.

It was only then I realized what a parallel there was

between that meeting and this one. Maybe Quinn and Fred had met for the same reason Rose and I were: to discuss who might have killed Jack and set the fires, with the hope of not being seen by that very person. Or people. There was still no telling if the killer and the arsonist were one and the same.

I sighed and pinched the bridge of my nose between my eyes. "I need a flowchart to keep track of all these meetings and confrontations." I looked at Rose again. "Thank you for telling me all of this. I don't think you had any reason to be scared about sharing what you learned."

Rose's wide eyes glittered in the bit of light that we had. "I was afraid of Ellis when Quinn first told me. I was worried he had killed Jack. But, now, it's Fred I'm afraid of. I'm pretty sure he's the killer."

"What makes you think that?"

"Because Fred came to the Grand today to see that rich real estate guy, Mr. Porter. They kept laughing, and Fred told him it was looking like all the obstacles were falling away."

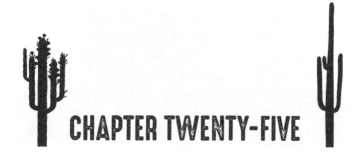

CHAPTER TWENTY-FIVE

Suddenly, I understood Rose's fear. She had good reason to be worried that Fred had, in fact, killed Jack.

"That's when I knew I had to be brave and talk to you," Rose continued.

I had already suspected Leland of setting the fires, and the meeting between him and Fred wasn't the first. The two of them had been celebrating in the saloon together, apparently happy about something.

Had that something been Jack's death?

And had Fred agreed to letting his own store be set on fire so it would be easier for Leland to buy the place? What would Fred even get out of such a deal?

"Another bizarre meeting," I mumbled.

"What?" Rose was giving me a confused look.

"Like I said, I need a flowchart to keep track of all the secret and not-so-secret meetings."

"I hope you and the police find the killer soon. I want this to be over with." Rose looked afraid again, but I knew she was thinking more of Quinn's security than her own.

"We all want that," I assured her.

Rose didn't have any more information, so I thanked her and told her what she had shared had been enormously helpful. It was ironic she had come to tell me about

Ellis and Fred threatening Jack, but the really insightful information had been about the apparent collaboration between Fred and Leland, instead.

Just what sort of obstacles falling away had Fred been referring to? In my mind, I saw Jack literally falling after getting conked on the head inside the bakery.

I waited until Rose had disappeared from sight before I called softly, "Malcolm? Theo?"

Even though I knew my friends weren't far away, I still jumped as Malcolm emerged from the darkness just a few feet from me. "Have you been there the whole time?" I asked.

"Yes." Malcolm's skeletal face stretched into a grin. "I told you that you wouldn't see me."

"You were close enough to hear what Rose said. What do you think?"

"I think she's right to be worried about Fred. It's strange, though, isn't it? The guy has been running the general store for years, minding his own business. He doesn't seem like the type to suddenly murder, especially over something as trivial as the rent price."

"It's not trivial to him. That's his living you're talking about."

"True. But consider how popular the general store is with tourists. I highly doubt Fred is struggling to pay his bills each month."

"A rent hike would likely affect someone like Chelsea a lot more," I agreed. "She can only bake so many things each day, while Fred could simply order more of the general store's most popular sellers."

Theo and Damien were converging on us, so Malcolm and I began to fill them in, but Theo raised a hand to stop us. "I'd much rather discuss this over a glass of blood."

"Yuck," I said.

"I bet you won't say yuck to a glass of wine," Damien guessed.

"White wine. I don't want it to look anything like what Theo is drinking."

In short order, the four of us were in the alley behind the coffee shop, and Clara's aunt was gazing at us through the small window in the metal door. Once she had verified we were members of the supernatural community, she opened the door for us and ushered us inside. As we descended the spiral staircase into the basement, she called, "I hope you're not here for long. There's still an arsonist out there!"

"Just a quick stop," Malcolm assured her. "Besides, the others are already patrolling." Zach, Malcolm told me in an aside, had headed right to Cowboy's Corral after seeing me safely to the bank.

I always enjoyed a visit to Under the Undertaker's. The cozy little nooks created by long strips of jewel-toned silk hanging from the ceiling gave the place an intimate feel, and the candlelight was relaxing.

The four of us sat on low stools around a small table. The bar was empty, but when our server came over, she waved at the vacant chairs happily. "Nightmare's supernatural community is out guarding the town, including this place. I may not get much in tips tonight, but it's worth the peace of mind."

Malcolm drank a club soda, saying he wanted a clear head before taking up his watch alongside Zach at the motel. I stuck to my decision to have a white wine, and Damien went for a snack instead of a cocktail. He tried to chew the bar's homemade potato chips quietly while Malcolm and I repeated the news Rose had relayed.

"Fred and Leland," Damien said. "What an unlikely pair, whether or not they killed anyone."

"I wonder if Leland made promises to Fred." Theo was staring thoughtfully into his glass. "He could have offered lower rent, or at the very least, no rent increase, if Fred would help him out."

"Or Leland could have told Fred he'd allow whatever changes he wanted to make to the general store," I said. "The display window had to be sacrificed, but maybe Fred wanted to redo it, anyway."

"It's also possible they both simply disliked Jack." Malcolm drained the last of his club soda and put the glass down with a firm thunk. "Surely Leland met with Jack before his demise, and he probably encountered a great deal of resistance."

We had talked ourselves past facts and into speculation, so there was no point in continuing the discussion. Malcolm offered to escort me back to the motel, since he was heading there, anyway. Damien and Theo were both heading out to their patrol areas for the night. I had offered to join Damien again, but he had insisted I go home and get some sleep.

When I walked into my bathroom to get ready for bed, I could see why Damien had sent me home. The dark underneath my eyes wasn't smudged pirate eyeliner.

I looked a lot perkier when I woke up on Tuesday morning. The face in the mirror was that of someone who had slept a solid eight hours. Once I was showered and dressed, I did some marketing work for the motel while I sipped my coffee. Most people were eating lunch already, while I was just beginning my day.

I got into a good rhythm with my work, and it was a rumble in my stomach that pulled me out of it. I was just thinking about making a sandwich, when there was a light knock on my door.

Damien was standing on my doorstep. "I'm glad to see I didn't wake you up."

"Are you hungry?" I asked as he came inside. "I can make us a late lunch while you fill me in on last night's watch."

"Lunch would be great, but you won't even get two pieces of bread onto the plate before I finish my report. I meant it when I texted you that we had a quiet night. No fires, and not one single shady person skulking around Nightmare in the wee hours."

"Maybe the arsonist is done with their handiwork," I said from my spot at the kitchen counter. "Fred did tell Leland the obstacles were falling away, and maybe there are none left."

"But we still don't know what those obstacles were, and how they relate to Leland," Damien pointed out.

"I need some food in my belly before we ponder all the possibilities."

We never got around to that pondering that because my phone rang just as we were finishing our sandwiches. It was Mama, who said, "Can you and Damien come up to the office, please?"

"How do you know Damien is here? Never mind. I should be used to the fact that you just seem to know things. We'll be right there."

We knew the reason we were being hailed to the office as soon as we spotted Nick's tow truck. He and Lucy were inside the office, talking to Mama.

"I'm guessing you have an update about the Vanishing Girls for us," I said to Lucy.

She turned to me with a look that was slightly sad. "They're gone."

"What do you mean, gone?" I looked between Lucy and Mama, but Mama just shook her head and shrugged.

"I saw Hazel on the playground at recess, and I asked her if the dead could help her and her friends, just like you said. But she told me no, the man who killed them isn't there anymore. His ghost is already gone, so there's nothing more they can do. And I said, 'Okay, I guess you don't have to worry about him then.' But Hazel said since he was gone, there was no reason for them to stay, either. She said thank you, and then"—Lucy made a *whoosh* noise —"all three were gone. Not just disappeared, but gone." She pressed a hand against her chest.

"They crossed over," Mama said gently. "That's good, Lucy. They're at peace now."

"Yeah, I guess." Lucy's mouth turned down. "I'll kind of miss seeing Hazel on the playground, but I'm glad I got to help. She said they were freed because I heard Lucille's message about them being hidden under the hill."

I reached down and took both of Lucy's hands. "That's right. Your work helped free them from the cave where they were trapped, and you helped them get the closure they needed so they could move on. We are so proud of you."

"I'm sad, but I also feel good. I want to help more ghosts."

"And you will," Mama said. "Ghosts will be able to sense your abilities, and they'll know they can communicate with you. They'll come to you for help. But, in the meantime, I think you've earned some ice cream for helping the Vanishing Girls."

"Wasn't the promise of ice cream what their killer used to lure them into his car?" Damien asked softly.

Mama looked horrified, but Lucy nodded firmly. "I'll have the ice cream for them!"

"How about we make it a girls' outing?" Mama gestured toward Nick and Damien. "The boys can mind the office while we go have a treat. Three girls having ice cream to honor the three Vanishing Girls!"

"That's a great idea!" Lucy's sadness lifted in an

instant, and she was bouncing on the balls of her feet as she led the way out the door.

The ice cream parlor was only two doors down from the bakery. A sign next to the door claimed the shop's vanilla ice cream had been Sheriff Connor McCrory's favorite treat. I hadn't even known ice cream parlors existed in the Wild West, so I would have to ask McCrory later if there was any truth to the claim.

Vanilla seemed like too boring of a flavor for honoring three ghosts, though, so we all opted for the wildest sundaes we could imagine. Mine was a salted caramel ice cream topped with chocolate sauce, chopped walnuts, whipped cream, and extra cherries.

Clara would have been so proud of me.

We squeezed around a small round table and dug into our sundaes with gusto. I had only made it halfway through mine when I saw Quinn walk inside. He looked surly, as usual, but when he glanced in our direction, Mama called him over in a loud, friendly voice. Quinn reluctantly came over, his expression wary.

"How's your mom doing? I was going to call her this afternoon." Even as Mama was saying that, I spotted Chelsea herself walking in the door, and as soon as she saw our group, she headed in our direction.

Quinn didn't see his mother since she was behind him, and he sneered. "I don't get it. Someone killed my ex-stepfather inside her bakery, then set the place on fire. I'm so mad that someone is doing this to her, but she's being super calm about it. She says we can't change what happened, so there's no reason to dwell on it."

"That's right," Chelsea said. Quinn looked startled, then embarrassed, and his cheeks reddened. "What happened, happened. It's history. Change is inevitable, and we have to accept it."

Chelsea's words were familiar ones, and I stared down at my half-eaten sundae while I thought back.

Ice cream.

The Vanishing Girls.

I put my spoon down and said quietly, "I think I just figured out who killed Jack."

CHAPTER TWENTY-SIX

Lucy gasped dramatically while the others just stared at me with open mouths. After a few moments, Mama leaned forward and whispered, "Who?" Sprinkles tumbled off her spoon, which was forgotten in her hand.

I glanced around. The ice cream parlor was full, and I didn't want anyone to overhear me. Plus, I wanted to run my theory past an expert because it was possibly a far-fetched one that was wildly off the mark. "I need to talk about it with Reyes first. Eat up, ladies, then we'll walk down to the police station."

"I'm going with you," Chelsea said. Quinn was nodding emphatically.

"I don't want to wait." Mama stood and grabbed her sundae bowl. She turned her face in the direction of the young woman doling out scoops at the counter. "I'll bring my dish back later this afternoon!"

Lucy giggled. "We can take the ice cream bowls?"

"We'll bring them back. Come on."

I had too much nervous energy swirling through me to even think of finishing my sundae, but I did have to smile at the sight of Mama and Lucy shoveling ice cream into their mouths while dodging tourists along the boardwalk. When I began to outpace both of them, I took a deep breath and forced my feet to slow down.

Chelsea and Quinn were trailing behind us, both looking anxious.

We reached the police station right as Lucy was taking her last bite of ice cream. I marched inside and was heading for the front desk when I heard the very man I was looking for. He was shouting. "I uphold the law, not building codes!"

I looked to see Reyes and Ellis standing toe to toe, both of them with angry expressions.

Mama was so startled she dropped her spoon into her bowl, and the clatter echoed throughout the room. Reyes looked over and narrowed his eyes at me. "Olivia, you have that look on your face. You've figured out who killed Jack Wiley."

I nodded.

"Let's hear it, then. Who do I need to arrest?"

In answer, I stretched out my arm and pointed at Ellis.

"What?" Chelsea said in a surprised voice.

"No way," Quinn added.

"Listen to the kid," Ellis said, turning his anger on me. "What a ridiculous accusation."

"You hated that new display window at the general store," I said. "Up until Fred installed it, the two of you were threatening Jack with various legal repercussions. You were doing it for history's sake, wanting Jack to do a better job caring for the buildings he owned, and Fred was doing it for the sake of his bank account, because he didn't want any rent increases. After Fred put that display window in, you were angry that Jack let it stay. He didn't care that it marred the historical accuracy of the general store. You love Chelsea's baked goods, and when you stopped into the bakery one morning, Jack was there. You saw your opportunity, and you attacked him."

Ellis crossed his arms over his chest. "Oh, really? And tell me, what did I supposedly attack him with?"

"I expect you did it with the brass lamp that was donated for the Nightmare Historic Society's fundraiser auction. I noticed it when we brought you the model skull. You'd collected the lamp from a donor, and I'm willing to bet it was in your hand when you went into the bakery."

I wasn't at all certain about the lamp, in fact, but I must have hit close to the mark, because Ellis blanched, and his chest heaved.

With that encouragement, I plowed ahead. "You killed Jack, and then you realized Leland Porter was interested in buying up historic places. He was vocal about wanting to make sweeping changes to them, including a lot of modernizations, so you wanted to scare him off. You set those fires hoping to deter him."

Ellis laughed sarcastically. "If I love historic places so much, then why would I ever set them on fire? Your logic doesn't make any sense, especially since my own hotel was torched."

"The dumpster was set on fire," I reminded Ellis, "and the damage to the hotel was minimal. But it achieved what you wanted it to: Leland realized he was being targeted. As for the bakery and general store fires, they were small and easy to contain. At the bakery, only the kitchen expansion out back was targeted. The burning mannequin at the general store only damaged that display window you hated. You set fire to the modern changes to those buildings. In fact, you told me you spent two hours writing a list of recommendations for the general store about how to return it to its historic look. You said it was on behalf of the historic society, but it was really for yourself in an effort to preserve Nightmare's history."

"Oh, Ellis," Chelsea said. She sounded heartbroken. "After everything you've done to support the bakery over the years. You did all this?"

Mama also seemed more sad than angry. "I was

convinced you were innocent. I guess my psychic senses need a tune-up."

Ellis was looking between the two women, and the anger seemed to die out of him. His shoulders sagged, and he squeezed his eyes shut. "How did you figure it out?"

"It all came down to history. Hazel, one of the Vanishing Girls, mentioned it first."

"Who?" Chelsea and Quinn chorused, but Reyes nodded. Either Justine had told him about the ghostly girls, or he had heard the urban legend about them.

"Then Chelsea herself mentioned it," I continued, "just now at the ice cream parlor. You can't change history, as both Hazel and Chelsea said. But you, Ellis, you wanted everything to stay exactly as it was. You killed Jack to protect the historic buildings he owned, then you tried to scare off Leland, who would have done even more harm to them."

Ellis sighed loudly as I continued. "Those fires were a way to undo what you perceived as improper changes to the old buildings you cherish so much. If you ruined the modern touches, they could be restored to their original state, as long as someone like you was there to give guidance. I'd guess you even called the fire department yourself, to make sure the fires didn't get out of control."

"I love this town," Ellis said. He gave Reyes a pleading look. "Nightmare has such an incredible history, and we can't let it be lost to real estate developers and careless landlords. I was just trying to protect this town and everything that makes it special."

Reyes shook his head sadly. "It's not the old buildings that make Nightmare special. It's the people who make this place what it is. It's a shame you can't see that. Ellis Upton, you're under arrest for the murder of Jack Wiley and three counts of arson."

As Reyes went through the process of arresting Ellis, I put an arm around Mama, who was staring at the scene with a mixture of shock and sadness.

When I felt a tug on my sleeve, I looked down to see Lucy, her eyes wide. "Miss Olivia, is it true that Hazel helped you figure everything out?"

"Yes."

Lucy grinned and stuck out her chin. "That means I helped solve this murder, too, because I'm the one who talked to Hazel. I guess that means someone has to buy me more ice cream!"

"The next sundae is on me," I promised. Then, I turned to Quinn. "There are a couple things I haven't been able to figure out. One of them is why you and Fred were arguing in the alley behind the general store in the middle of the night."

It was the first time since we'd originally met that I had seen Quinn looking something other than angry or embarrassed. He actually laughed. "First of all, how did you know about that? The whole point of meeting at that time was so no one would see us. He and I had been making vague accusations to each other, so we finally agreed to meet and hash it out. We both accused the other of being the arsonist. Fred had been buddying up to that rich guy, Leland, and I thought he was setting the fires so no one else would want to deal with the repairs."

"I suspected something similar," I admitted. "I knew Fred and Leland were scheming somehow, but I couldn't figure out how Fred might benefit from ensuring Leland could buy those buildings without any trouble."

"It came down to greed," Quinn said simply. "According to Fred, Leland was promising to modernize the general store, saying there was no need to worry about historic guidelines. Leland told him there were always loopholes. Fred liked the idea of being able to add more windows to the front of the store, and maybe even a second level so he could sell more stuff."

"So, when Fred told Leland that obstacles were falling away, he was probably referring to the fires frightening off other potential buyers," I said thoughtfully. "But neither man was actually setting them. Ellis was trying to preserve history, but instead, he was making it easier for Leland to scoop up those buildings. No one else would want to deal with the fire damage or the threat of the arsonist striking again."

"Well, I sure hope the bakery is up and running again soon," Mama said. "I miss my cinnamon rolls."

"Don't worry," Chelsea said. "Sid is going to try to buy the building. All he has to do is outbid Leland."

"You know," I said, "I had Sid on my suspect list, too."

"Honestly, I figured you would. His temper and his dislike of Jack made him look pretty guilty. Fred's accusations certainly didn't help."

"But he's a good guy," Quinn put in. "He treats Mom like she deserves to be treated."

"That's good to hear," I said sincerely. "I wonder who will end up buying the general store? Fred might still get his wish of modernizing the place."

Mama planted her hands on her hips. "Hopefully, Mr. Porter will decide there's too much drama in this town for his taste, and he'll take his money somewhere else. I can't wait to tell him we're not going to sell the motel to him."

Chelsea and Quinn thanked both Mama and me, then headed out. As they went, I heard Chelsea say something about making a celebratory batch of muffins.

Mama took Lucy's hand. "Now that the Cowboy's Corral private investigators have wrapped up the case, it's time for us to go, too."

We had only made it as far as the sidewalk, when my phone buzzed, alerting me to a text message. It was from Damien, and it read simply, *Get to the Sanctuary ASAP. Bring Mama and Lucy.*

CHAPTER TWENTY-SEVEN

We walked as quickly as Mama could go in the direction of her car. She sent Lucy ahead to return our bowls to the ice cream parlor, and in a few minutes, we were racing to the Sanctuary. Lucy squealed with delight every time Mama took a corner too quickly.

Mama had to drive slowly once we turned onto the dirt lane that led to the front of the Sanctuary, and she kept driving onto the cracked and overgrown circular driveway, finally coming to a stop right at the building's entrance. Malcolm was there, and he looked excited but not worried. I felt my body relax as I climbed out of the car.

"I called Damien as soon as it started," he said. "Don't worry, Mama, your son is still holding things down at the motel."

"As soon as what started?" I asked.

"It's Baxter. We think he's trying to communicate something, but we don't know what. We're hoping one of you can figure it out."

As we walked toward the dining room, Malcolm gave us a few more details. "We've been leaving the door of the birdcage open, figuring Baxter would want to fly around. So far, he hasn't. He just sits there and watches all of us. Until about thirty minutes ago, at least, when he let out the loudest squawk you can imagine and soared out of the cage. He's been flying around the dining room since then, sometimes dive-bombing people."

Mama put a hand out over Lucy's head. "Is it even safe for us to go in there?"

Malcolm nodded. "He's not actually hitting anyone. It's like he's trying to alert us to something, but we don't understand."

When we walked into the dining room, everyone except the vampires, who would be asleep until sundown, was gathered together. A few were sitting down, but most were standing up, their eyes following the beautiful phoenix as he zoomed in circles overhead. Felipe was standing up on his hind legs, his front paws extended and his eyes fixed on Baxter.

We were just in time so see Baxter dive down and swoop close to Gunnar's head. "I don't speak phoenix!" Gunnar said. He sounded frustrated.

"It would be much easier if we could speak bird," Morgan agreed.

"Sadly, there is no magic for that," Madge added.

Maida didn't chime in. She was too busy giggling as she watched Baxter's antics. Lucy ran straight to her and shouted, "I love your socks!" The two of them immediately struck up a conversation about pink accessories.

Mama and I took up a spot on either side of Damien. "Any ideas?" I asked.

Seraphina, whose tank was nearby, overheard me. "There's nothing about this kind of behavior in Baxter's phoenix guide. Damien, you should try talking to him."

Damien looked uncertain as he raised his face toward the bird. "Dad? Can you understand me?"

Apparently, Baxter could understand, because he angled down toward Damien, then came to rest on the table near where we were standing.

"We think you're trying to tell us something," Damien said. "But we can't understand what you want. Is there something we need to do for you?"

Baxter squawked so loudly I clamped my hands over my ears.

"Okay, I think that's a yes. Can you tell us in some way other than flying in circles?"

In answer, Baxter lifted into the air again. I expected him to begin flying around overhead, but instead, he sped toward the dining room door and circled in front of it.

I wasn't far from the door, so I quickly closed the distance and opened it. Baxter flew right out the door and down the hallway.

I hurried after him with Damien on my heels. Behind me, I could hear everyone else following, too.

Baxter led us to Damien's office. Which, I reminded myself, was really Baxter's. Once there, he tapped his beak against a dark-green book on one of the shelves.

Damien, Mama, Lucy, and Malcolm had all followed me into the office. As Damien slid the hardcover book from the shelf, I heard Zach's voice from the doorway. "We can't all fit in. I'll let everyone out here know what's happening."

The book had gold lettering that read *Nightmare, Arizona: From Boomtown to Tourist Town.*

"Nightmare history," Mama said. "That seems to be our theme today. Maybe Baxter has also figured out who killed Jack."

Damien glanced at me. "What?"

"We'll tell you once this is all over with," I assured him. "But, yes, we found the murderer and the arsonist, who happened to be the same person."

Damien looked like he wanted more details, but Baxter was beating his wings madly to stay near the book, his beak tapping the cover impatiently. "Okay, Dad, okay. I'll turn the pages, and you show me when I've gotten to whatever you want me to see."

Damien went behind his desk and opened the book on it. Baxter settled onto the desk, too, watching intently as Damien slowly began to turn the pages.

It wasn't until page two hundred forty-six that Baxter leaned down and firmly planted the tip of his beak on the page.

"What's this part of the book about?" I asked, leaning over the desk and trying to read upside down.

"Something about the copper-rich soil creating mystical conditions," Damien said as he perused the text. "A legend about a mineshaft that has whatever kind of ore the miner is seeking...and something about an alleged energy well."

Baxter squawked, the sound echoing in the confines of the office.

"Energy well!" Lucy echoed. "Like that ghost pool we went to!"

"Is that what you want?" Damien asked Baxter. "Do you want us to take you to the energy spring where you used to take Tanner and McCrory?"

Another squawk was, we decided, a yes.

"Seraphina mentioned a power transfer would be necessary for Baxter's transformation to human form," I remembered.

"Count us in!" I felt a cold waft of air against the back of my neck, and I looked over my shoulder to see Tanner.

Damien glanced at the antique clock on the desk. "It will be dark in a couple of hours. We're closed tonight, so everyone can join us who wants to, and we'll wait until it's fully dark out so Gunnar can safely go without being seen."

"Plus, that means Theo and Mori can join us," I noted.

"That, too." Damien looked at Baxter with a raised eyebrow. "Does that plan work for you?"

The phoenix extended its shimmery red-orange wings, then settled into a more relaxed position.

"Now, we wait," Damien said. We all trooped back to the dining room. Even Baxter came with us, flying at a more sedate pace this time. Felipe trotted along underneath him, still staring intently up at the bird.

As I slid onto a bench at one of the dining room tables, I heard Fiona say, "How about a game of poker?" A few people responded enthusiastically to that idea, and she led them to a table a short distance away.

Malcolm announced, "I'll whip up a batch of Victorian funeral cookies while we wait."

"Not quite cinnamon rolls, but okay," Mama commented to me. "I'll call Nick and tell him we're sticking around here for a while. Where is Lucy, anyway?"

I pointed to a far corner. "She and Maida are distracting Felipe so he doesn't keep trying to get Baxter."

Damien didn't sit down the entire time we waited. Even when Malcolm came out of the kitchen and handed around still-warm cookies, Damien ate while he paced. I said as many comforting things as I could think of, but he was still anxious to know what was going to happen when we arrived at the energy spring.

When the vampires woke, we filled them in on the latest development with Baxter. "Oh, and also," Mama said, "Olivia caught the killer."

Damien stopped his pacing and looked abashed. "Olivia, I'm so sorry. I totally forgot to ask for more details. It's just that—" Damien gestured to where Baxter was perched on the table.

"I know. It's okay."

"Did my delicious dinner date do it?" Mori asked.

"He did not. Jack Wiley was killed by Ellis Upton."

"The manager of the Nightmare Grand?" Clara had a

cookie in each hand, and she was speaking around the whole one she had just shoved into her mouth.

"The one and only. He set the fires, too." I repeated all the pieces I had put together that made me realize Ellis was both the killer and the arsonist.

"I'm calling Luis right now," Justine said.

"Make it fast," I advised as I eyed Baxter, who had stretched upward to his full length and extended his wings. "I think he's ready to hit the road."

"I'll talk while Clara drives." Justine was already pulling out her phone.

Even Seraphina went with us to the energy spring. Fiona loaded the siren into her van, rolling the water tank up a ramp and into the back.

I rode with Damien, who was happy to be behind the wheel of his Corvette again. He had picked up the birdcage, telling Baxter we were going to the energy spring, but Baxter had soared out the dining room door and waited at the entrance to the Sanctuary until someone opened one of the doors. He had flown out and quickly disappeared from view.

Gunnar had taken off after the phoenix, promising he would keep an eye on Baxter until the rest of us could arrive by vehicle.

We had quite the caravan heading to the energy spring. Two vampires, two ghosts, three witches, a siren, a banshee, a psychic, a chupacabra, and more, all following a phoenix to a mysterious concentration of energy in the desert.

"If I haven't mentioned it lately," I told Damien as we approached the crossroads at the gallows, "I really love my job."

"Turn right," Tanner instructed from behind me.

"I'm telling you, it's faster to go straight." McCrory gave a long-suffering sigh.

The ghosts continued to bicker about the correct route, even as Damien effortlessly guided his car to the right spot. We parked and made the short walk to the energy spring, where Baxter was flying in circles. I couldn't see or feel the energy welling up from the ground, but I knew he must be circling its epicenter.

It felt surreal to stand there in the desert landscape with every single person from the Sanctuary, plus Mama and Lucy. The light from the half-moon and the brilliant stars gave just enough illumination for me to see the hopeful expressions on everyone's faces. I gripped Damien's hand tightly as we watched Baxter's body begin to emit its own light.

Soon, the entire phoenix was glowing. As Baxter got brighter, his body took on a golden-white hue. The shadows around us fled, and it felt like daylight had returned.

The light became too bright for me, and I threw up a hand to shield my eyes. Others were doing the same, and the last thing I saw before I had to shut my eyes tight against the searing light was Malcolm, who was running toward Baxter while shrugging his coat off his shoulders.

There was silence, and then I heard a man say, "Thank you, Malcolm. Creating clothes out of thin air is one thing I can't do."

I blinked my eyes open, but the blinding light was gone. So was the phoenix. Instead, I saw Malcolm standing next to a man with black hair and a wide grin below a bushy mustache. He was wearing Malcolm's long black coat, and he was just finishing buttoning it up.

Damien stepped forward. His hand was still tightly holding mine, so I was pulled along with him. "Dad?" Damien's voice was nearly inaudible.

Baxter looked at Damien proudly. "My son. It's so

good to see you." He moved toward us, and Damien finally dropped my hand as he and his father embraced.

I heard a loud sniff to my left, and I looked over to see all three witches dabbing their cheeks with white handkerchiefs. Seraphina had hoisted herself as high as she could on the edge of her mobile water tank, and she was openly crying.

It was only then I realized I was crying, too.

Baxter and Damien stepped back from each other. "I know I haven't always been a good dad," Baxter began.

Damien waved a hand. "You did the best you could. We found Mom's diary, so we know about her putting herself into a spell to keep me safe. It helped explain why you were so protective of me as a kid."

"I helped keep you safe, and then you helped me recover myself." Lucille's ghost appeared next to Baxter, her form much stronger than it had been when we had first taken her to the energy spring. At a glance, the only sign she was a ghost was the soft shimmer around her.

"Look at us," Baxter said, beaming at his wife. "Our family is together again."

"Great-aunt Lucille!" Lucy cried. She raised her arms, her fingers spread wide as she did a celebratory dance. Beside her, Mama stood with both hands pressed over her heart.

"You helped me, too, Lucy," Lucille said. "As did Olivia. Your combined powers served as a catalyst for my consciousness."

Baxter looked around at everyone. We were all silent, still too in awe of what we were witnessing to react. "And when I say our family is together again," he said loudly, "I mean all of us. I'm so happy to be home, and I know each one of you played a part in my recovery. Thank you."

Felipe lifted his head and yowled. With a laugh, Fiona opened her mouth and wailed, keeping her pitch and volume well below her usual banshee level. Zach joined in with a howl only a werewolf could achieve. Soon, we were all cheering, shouting, and clapping.

Once the celebration had quieted down, Damien looked at his mother. "Are you ready to go home, Mom?"

Lucille smiled contentedly. "I'm with my husband, my son, and all the people I love. I'm already home."

EPILOGUE

"I can't decide if it's genius or the most ridiculous idea I've ever heard," Damien said.

"Justine said we needed to find ways to boost summer business, when there are fewer tourists coming to Nightmare." I gestured toward the thermostat on the wall of the dining room. "The Chills and Thrills theme would promote both the haunt and our excellent air-conditioning."

Damien made a noise of mock frustration and turned to Baxter. "Dad, are you sure you don't want this job back?"

Baxter laughed. "No, thank you. I'm retired. I was way past retirement age to begin with, and I want to spend time with your mom."

The one thing Baxter refused to tell us was how old he really was. When he said he was past retirement age, the years were quite possibly measured in triple digits.

Lucille was a few feet away, chatting with Fiona and Seraphina. In the two weeks since Baxter had returned to his human form, Lucille had continued looking as vibrant as Tanner and McCrory. With regular trips to the energy spring, Lucille speculated she was back for good. It wasn't quite the same as having a body, she said, but it was good enough.

Every day since Baxter's return had been a joyful one. The people at the Sanctuary were enjoying catching up with him, and I was eagerly getting to know him. I was also bonding with Lucille, who was a warm, loving woman, just like her sister.

"Olivia and I are going to do some practicing of our supernatural skills later," Damien said. "As soon as I talk her out of her oddball marketing idea for summer tourists."

"I'm going to conjure you telling me it's a fantastic idea," I joked.

"You'd better," said Justine. She and Clara were sitting at the other end of the table, going over some logistics before that night's family meeting began. "I already started designing flyers to post around High Noon Boulevard."

"See?" I said as I lifted a cinnamon roll from the nearby pastry box. "They understand the importance of staying cool."

Instead of biting into the cinnamon roll, I looked at it thoughtfully. I must have gazed longer than I realized, because Damien said, "Don't worry. They taste just as good as the ones from the bakery."

"Oh, it's not that," I said.

The staff at the Nightmare Grand had felt awful that their manager was responsible for the bakery being unusable at the moment, and they had offered to let Chelsea use their kitchen until the bakery was repaired. Chelsea had readily agreed.

I finally looked up. "I'm thinking about the first cinnamon rolls I ever had from Bake in the Day. When I came to Nightmare, Mama had a box of them at Cowboy's Corral, and she gave me some. I was so broke that those rolls were a couple of my meals. I was reluctant to tell her, but Mama sensed I was in dire straits."

"Of course she did," Baxter said with a chuckle. "She

always claimed to be the so-called normal one, but the rest of us knew better."

"She took good care of me in those early days in Nightmare. She still does."

"And you take good care of her," Damien said. "Plus, you make sure she gets plenty of excitement."

"Hopefully, the most excitement we have in the near future is the homecoming party for Baxter and Lucille." To emphasize my point, I took a giant bite of the cinnamon roll.

Malcolm swept into the room, his coat trailing behind him. Zach followed, and the two looked like they were having a serious conversation. They walked right up to us, but Malcom hesitated, looking from Damien to Baxter.

Baxter hooked a thumb in Damien's direction. "He's in charge now."

"Zach and I have been working on a plan in case the Night Runners come back," Malcolm said.

We had been in such a celebratory mood about Baxter's recovery that it had been easy to ignore the reason he had gone missing in the first place. The Night Runners, a faction that operated on the supernatural black market, had known he was a phoenix, and they had taken him for the magical elements he could provide, such as feathers and ashes.

When Baxter had first gone missing, Malcolm tried tracking him. He had found Baxter's footprints along a dirt road, until the tracks had just stopped. It was only later we learned Baxter was a phoenix, and after his recovery, Baxter told us the full tale of his kidnapping. The Night Runners members who had taken him had gotten their hands on a dark-magic spell that made Baxter revert from his human form to his natural state as a bird. As soon as the spell had been cast, they grabbed Baxter before he had even figured out what was going on.

Just as Malcolm had been the most proactive about finding Baxter in the first place, he was now leading the charge to make sure Baxter remained safe. We didn't know if the Night Runners would try to take him again, but if so, we would all be ready.

"The moon reaches full tomorrow night," Zach said. "I'm trying to finalize the details of our security plan before I transform." He looked serene instead of grumpy, since he was looking forward to three days of running around as a wolf.

Baxter waved a hand. "Oh, don't worry about it too much. Tanner and McCrory can keep an eye on me while you're in wolf form. Besides, don't forget that my home is well-guarded against supernatural creatures. The iron door on Sonny's Folly Mine keeps even you at bay, Zach."

I glanced at Damien, who had seemed relieved to move out of the old copper mine so Baxter and Lucille could have their former home to themselves. Damien was currently living in one of the apartments above us, and he had told me at least three times how great it was to have windows again.

"Theo wants to help with security, too," I noted. "Damien, you thought my Chills and Thrills marketing plan was ridiculous? Wait until you hear Theo's plan to make any intruders walk the plank of the prop pirate ship. He and Mori will wake up in a few hours, so he can fill you in." I glanced at my watch to check if my estimate was correct, and I jumped to my feet with a gasp. "I have to go! I promised Mama I'd pick Lucy up at school and bring her back here for her weekly lesson with Vivian."

"I'll walk you out," Damien said, rising smoothly from the bench. "I think Malcolm and Zach have things well under control."

We passed Gunnar in the hallway on our walk to the front doors, and he pointed a clawed finger at me. "You need a trim. Tomorrow, arrive early, and I'll get your hair in shape before work."

"Thanks!" I called after him.

The day was warm, and it was easy to feel how quickly we were rushing toward summertime and the kind of desert heat that would make me wilt. At the moment, though, the temperature wasn't too bad.

When we reached my car, Damien spun me toward him and wrapped his arms around me. He leaned down and kissed me, lingering longer than usual. "I'll see you soon. I've got an appointment with Emmett in a bit."

"As long as you don't buy a mine to convert, like your dad did," I teased. "You need lots of sunshine."

"Emmett says he has a list of places for me to look at." Damien's green eyes slid away and focused on the dirt below us. "But, I thought... Well, maybe you should help me choose a place. In case the house I buy is your home someday, too."

Damien brought his gaze back to my face, and even in the bright sunshine, I could see the soft glow in his eyes.

I knew I was blushing, but I was smiling, too. "I'm not too picky. I want a place that doesn't have decades-old shag carpet, and we need a fenced backyard so Felipe can run around when Mori brings him to visit."

"We'll also need a saltwater pool for Seraphina."

"And a cemetery for Fiona!"

Damien laughed. "It will be the weirdest, most wonderful home in Nightmare."

I shook my head and looked over at the looming gray stone building that was Nightmare Sanctuary Haunted House. "No. That's already right here."

A NOTE FROM THE AUTHOR

Reader, thank you for coming on this journey to Nightmare, Arizona, with me. It's been 10 books and more than half a million words since Olivia's car broke down, leaving her with no job, no money, and nowhere to live. I'm so grateful you stuck by her side as she solved murders, made friends, and built a new life in Nightmare.

Is this *The End* for Olivia? For now, yes. But don't worry: I have plans for another novella, several short stories, and some other surprises. Nightmare will always be here, waiting for you whenever you need an escape.

Just watch out for that so-called "dog."

Eternally Yours,

Beth

P.S. You can keep up with my latest book news, get fun freebies, and more by signing up for my newsletter at BethDolgner.com!

If you enjoyed Nightmare, you'll love Foxfire Haven!

Spells and Subterfuge
Crones of a Feather Paranormal Cozy Mysteries #1

A reluctant witch, a haunted funeral home, and a dead body. Welcome home, Hazel.

Hazel Underwood has returned to her magical hometown of Foxfire Haven, Washington, with her tail between her legs.

A metaphorical tail, of course. Witches don't have tails.

While renovating the old funeral home she inherited from her uncle, Hazel stumbles on a dead body stashed underneath the hearse. Who wanted the delivery-truck driver dead, and how did he wind up in Hazel's garage? Chief Constable Hightower thinks Hazel might have killed Steve with her magic, and she's determined to prove the handsome old curmudgeon wrong.

Suspects range from a beautiful vampire with a passion for potions to the garden store gnome, but as Hazel closes in on solving the murder, she learns there's another mystery to unravel. What happened to Hazel's uncle in his final years to turn him into an obsessed treasure-hunter? And does his story tie into Steve's murder?

Hazel will have to team up with her witchy new roommates to catch a killer, stand up to judgmental small-town locals, and get her magic back on track. Who knew midlife could be so complicated?

The Crones of a Feather paranormal cozy mystery series is about starting over at midlife, magic, and building a sisterhood with strong, inspiring women. If the Golden Girls were witches, they'd be crones of a feather, too.

ACKNOWLEDGMENTS

My beta readers have stuck with me through all 10 books in this series. Kristine, Sabrina, Alex, David, Lisa, and Mom: thank you, thank you, thank you. Lia at Your Best Book Editor and Trish at Blossoming Pages are my editor heroes. Jena at BookMojo gave me a gorgeous cover, and Nikki at The Madd Formatter made the inside beautiful. The final group to see a book before it meets the world are my ARC readers, and I am so grateful for their enthusiastic support.

ABOUT THE AUTHOR

Beth Dolgner writes paranormal fiction and nonfiction. Her interest in things that go bump in the night really took off on a trip to Savannah, Georgia, so it's fitting that her first series—Betty Boo, Ghost Hunter—takes place in that spooky city. Beth also writes paranormal nonfiction, including her first book, *Georgia Spirits and Specters*, which is a collection of Georgia ghost stories.

Beth and her husband, Ed, live in Tucson, Arizona. They're close enough to Tombstone that Beth can easily visit its Wild West street and watch staged shootouts, all in the name of research for the Nightmare, Arizona series.

Beth also enjoys giving presentations on Victorian death and mourning traditions as well as Victorian Spiritualism. She has been a volunteer at an historic cemetery, a ghost tour guide, and a paranormal investigator.

Keep up with Beth and sign up for her newsletter at BethDolgner.com.

BOOKS BY BETH DOLGNER

The Crones of a Feather Series

Paranormal Cozy Mystery

Spells and Subterfuge

Divination and Deceit

Manifesting and Mischief

The Nightmare, Arizona Series

Paranormal Cozy Mystery

Homicide at the Haunted House

Drowning at the Diner

Slaying at the Saloon

Murder at the Motel

Poisoning at the Party

Headless at Halloween (Novella)

Clawing at the Corral

Axing at the Antique Store

Fatality at the Festival

Terminated at the Trailhead

Body at the Bakery

The Betty Boo, Ghost Hunter Series

Romantic Urban Fantasy

Ghost of a Threat

Ghost of a Whisper

Ghost of a Memory

Ghost of a Hope

The Eternal Rest Bed and Breakfast Series

Paranormal Cozy Mystery

Sweet Dreams

Late Checkout

Picture Perfect

Destination Wedding (Novella)

Scenic Views

Breakfast Included

Groups Welcome

Quiet Nights

Halloween Vibes (Novella)

Manifest

Young Adult Steampunk

A Talent for Death

Young Adult Urban Fantasy

Nonfiction

Georgia Spirits and Specters

Everyday Voodoo

Made in the USA
Monee, IL
01 June 2025

18539166R10132